COUNTY
LIBRARY

DARK SHADOWS

Other books by Joan Lingard

Younger fiction

THE FREEDOM MACHINE
HANDS OFF OUR SCHOOL!
FRYING AS USUAL

Fiction

TUG OF WAR
BETWEEN TWO WORLDS
NIGHT FIRES
LIZZIE'S LEAVING
THE GUILTY PARTY
RAGS AND RICHES
GLAD RAGS
THE FILE ON FRAULEIN BERG
THE GOOSEBERRY
SNAKE AMONG THE SUNFLOWERS
STRANGERS IN THE HOUSE
THE WINTER VISITOR

The Maggie *books*

THE CLEARANCE
THE RESETTLING
THE PILGRIMAGE
THE REUNION

The Kevin and Sadie *books* (in reading order)

THE TWELFTH DAY OF JULY
ACROSS THE BARRICADES
INTO EXILE
A PROPER PLACE
HOSTAGES TO FORTUNE

Joan Lingard

DARK SHADOWS

Hamish Hamilton • London

HAMISH HAMILTON LTD

Published by the Penguin Group
Penguin Books Ltd, 27 Wrights Lane, London W8 5TZ, England
Penguin Putnam Inc., 375 Hudson Street, New York, New York 10014, USA
Penguin Books Australia Ltd, Ringwood, Victoria, Australia
Penguin Books Canada Ltd, 10 Alcorn Avenue, Toronto, Ontario, Canada M4V 3B2
Penguin Books (NZ) Ltd, Private Bag 102902, NSMC Auckland, New Zealand

Penguin Books Ltd, Registered Offices: Harmondsworth, Middlesex, England

First published 1998
1 3 5 7 9 10 8 6 4 2

Set in 12.5/14pt Monotype Bembo
Typeset by Rowland Phototypesetting Ltd,
Bury St Edmunds, Suffolk
Printed in England by Clays Ltd, St Ives plc

British Library Cataloguing in Publication Data
A CIP catalogue record for this book is available from the British Library

ISBN 0-241-13774-8

For the other seven
and their children and grandchildren

ONE

Jess and Laurie Magowan were first cousins, and the same age, fifteen, but they'd never met until that Saturday night in Belfast. They met by chance.

Jess had gone to a music club for teenagers with Neal O'Shea, a cousin on her mother's side. Towards the end of the evening the MC made an announcement that made her sit up.

'Please give a big hand to Miss Laurie Magowan!'

'Laurie Magowan,' she murmured, but Neal didn't hear. He was too busy clapping. Jess thought he fancied Laurie from the moment she walked on the stage.

The clapping died and Laurie began to sing. She had the kind of voice that made everyone stop talking to listen. The applause afterwards was boisterous. People stamped their feet and whistled. The singer smiled and blushed. They shouted for an encore and she was persuaded to sing again.

When she'd stepped down and gone to join a couple of boys at a table near the front, Neal turned to Jess and said, 'She's brilliant!'

'Does she remind you of anyone?'

Neal looked puzzled.

'What about my father?' said Jess. Her father was blond and blue-eyed, like the singer. She herself had dark hair and dark eyes, and took after her mother. All the O'Sheas were dark.

'You don't think she's related to you?'

'She could be my cousin.'

'On the other side?'

'Obviously not on yours!'

Jess couldn't take her eyes off Laurie. She only half listened to the next act, the last on the bill. She was too busy thinking about her newly found cousin, for she was fairly certain it must be her.

At the end she got up quickly and headed for the foyer. Laurie was already out there, talking to an older man. Her father! Jess felt an echo of recognition: he was the spitting image of her own father. And spitting would probably be the right word for them if they were ever to meet again!

Laurie and her father talked for a minute or two and then she took something out of her bag, putting her back to the crowd. Jess thought it might be money but she couldn't quite see. Laurie's father pocketed whatever it was and departed. He didn't walk as straight or as vigorously as his brother. It was possible he had a drink or two in him.

Jess went up to Laurie before anyone else could corner her.

'I just wanted to tell you I thought you were fantastic.'

'Oh, thanks.' Laurie sounded rather shy.

Jess pressed on. 'I wonder if you could be the daughter of Ed Magowan by any chance?'

Laurie glanced instinctively towards the door. 'Why, yes.' She was guarded now.

'Would he have a brother, Tommy?'

'Well, yes, he does, but –' But they're not on speaking terms. She didn't have to say it.

'I'm Tommy's daughter, Jess.'

'You're not!'

'Cross my heart!'

'So we're –'

'Cousins!'

Laurie looked stunned.

They were joined then by the two boys who had been at her table.

'Dave,' said Laurie hesitantly, 'this is our cousin Jess Magowan. Jess, this is my brother, Dave. And Barney Dunlop.' That was the second boy.

Laurie's brother let out a long whistle. But he didn't get the chance to say anything before Neal interrupted with the news that Jess's father was waiting outside in the car.

'Better not miss your chariot,' said Dave then. Laurie shot him an annoyed look but he didn't pay any attention. He was regarding Neal, sizing him up. 'Don't tell me this is another cousin! They're dropping out the skies like bird shit!'

'My cousin, not yours!' Jess looked Dave straight in the eye. She wasn't going to be terrorized by this smart alec! 'This is Neal O'Shea.' She pronounced his second name clearly and defiantly. It was a Catholic surname, predominantly.

'An O'Shea!' Dave laughed, making a noise like a drain gurgling. 'Certainly no relation of ours then!'

'Oh, belt up!' said Laurie quietly.

'Tell Dad I'm just coming, would you, Neal?' said Jess.

He went off, after giving Dave a backward, angry look. Another minute or two and they might have had a scuffle on their hands. The two girls edged away from the boys.

'Don't pay any attention to my brother,' said Laurie. 'He's got a big mouth.'

'Don't worry your head about it.' Jess hesitated, then said, 'I was thinking it would be nice if we could meet sometime. Just the two of us. Would you like to?' When she wanted to do something she made up her mind quickly but she could see that Laurie wasn't like that. She had a cautious look on her, which reminded Jess of her own father.

'Well . . .' Laurie began. Her brother was right behind her.

'Give us a buzz if you feel like it,' said Jess casually. 'We're in the book. In Holywood.'

They said goodbye and Jess left. Neal was in the foyer reading a notice about a song-writing competition for under-eighteen-year-olds. He would be eighteen in four months' time.

'You'd just get under the wire,' said Jess.

'You like writing poems,' he said. And he liked composing melodies. 'So what about it?'

'Trouble is neither of us can sing all that well!' Jess didn't give the competition more than a moment's thought at that point. She knew her father would be getting restless.

He was parked right in front of the door.

'Took your time, didn't you?' he said.

Neal got in the back, Jess in the front.

'Dad,' she said, 'you'll never guess who I met tonight?'

Her news caused a small explosion. She was glad they weren't driving along the road.

'What are you getting so worked up for?' she demanded. 'The girl's done nothing to you.'

'I don't want you associating with that lot!'

'That *lot*? Aren't they your family?'

Tommy Magowan didn't answer. He revved up the engine and they took off like a rocket, causing a car coming up behind to honk furiously at them.

Neal was saying nothing. He was more diplomatic than Jess, or, as he would have put it, he knew when to keep his mouth shut. He worked as a mechanic in his uncle's garage so he had to be able to bite his tongue when necessary. But he was fond of his Uncle Tommy. He'd been like a father to him ever since his own father was killed in a pub bombing.

They crossed Albert Bridge and turned into the Short Strand, where Neal lived with his mother and grandfather. The Short Strand was a solid Republican area. Grandpa O'Shea was a solid Republican. He painted his kerb green, white and orange, which kept him occupied but irritated Neal and his mother.

They lived in one of the newer houses. They were terraced and not all that large but they had neat front gardens. As soon as the car pulled up the door opened and out came Neal's mother. She'd been at the window for the past hour. Every time Neal was a few minutes late she imagined the worst. She'd been anxious ever since her husband was killed. And who could blame her! Jess knew that but thought it was a bit heavy on Neal at times.

'Are you coming in a minute?' her aunt called from the doorstep.

'We'll need to be getting back, Maureen,' said Tommy. 'Maeve'll be wondering where we are. You know what you women are like.'

Maureen gave him a weak smile. Neal thanked his uncle for the lift and off he went up the path. By this time Grandpa O'Shea had come to the door to see what was going on. He was a fierce-looking old devil with bushy white eyebrows that met in the middle and sharp, dark eyes, slightly hooded, like a hawk's.

Jess and her father waved goodbye and set off for home, taking the bypass, which meant they avoided the city streets. They lived about five miles from the centre.

From their house on the hill they could look down on Belfast Lough. It was peaceful up here. The house was large and detached, with a spacious, mature garden surrounding it. Tommy parked his car in the garage alongside his wife's smaller one.

Maeve Magowan was in the sitting room with their son, Danny. They'd been arguing. Danny had been having a lot of trouble with his asthma and hadn't been at school for months. The doctor had said he was fit to go back in a week or so but Danny was disputing it.

Mother and son broke off from their row as Tommy and Jess came in.

Jess was still bursting with her piece of news.

'Mum,' she said, 'I met my cousin Laurie tonight. Uncle Ed's daughter!'

'The famous Uncle Ed?' said Danny.

'Infamous, more like!' said their father, before starting in on Jess. 'How many times do I have to tell you I want nothing to do with that family!'

'It is your family!'

'It hasn't been that for twenty years!'

'But you didn't fall out with Laurie! She wasn't even born then.'

'It was their fault, madam! Don't you forget that!'

Fault, fault, fault! Jess wanted to cover her ears.

'It takes two to quarrel,' she said, though more than two had been involved. 'Depends who started it.'

'They did,' said her father with finality.

'You give me a pain,' she said, and left the room.

'Stay away from them, do you hear!' her father shouted after her.

'How could I not hear?' she muttered.

Lying in bed with the open curtains letting in the moonlight, she stared at the shadows on the ceiling. They said the past cast long shadows over the present. It was certainly true in this province. And it was true in her family. Their shadows were not only long, but dark.

TWO

Laurie had known that her father had a brother called Tommy and that they'd fallen out over Tommy's marriage to Maeve O'Shea. It was past history, and she'd never given it much thought, until that night she met Tommy's daughter.

She had been conscious of the girl with the long, dark hair and wide, dark eyes staring intently at her while she was performing. She had noticed her too, afterwards, in the foyer when her father was talking to her.

Her father was telling her he'd just happened to be passing. As if he expected her to believe that! He was avoiding her eye, rattling the coins in his trouser pocket. Eventually he came out with the real purpose of his visit.

'Couldn't lend us a tenner, could you, Laurie? I seem to have left myself short.'

He was always short, had been since he'd been laid off from the shipyard a few years back. Laurie sighed and took out her purse. She'd been paid forty pounds for her performance. They didn't pay the first time a performer went on but if they liked you and asked you back they did. She gave him ten pounds.

'Ta, love. You're a great girl. I'll pay you back when my ship comes in.'

As soon as he'd taken himself off Jess came up. When she said who she was Laurie was taken aback. And when Jess asked if she'd like to meet again she didn't know what to say. Jess saw that and eased off, for which Laurie was glad. She needed time to get used to the idea.

After Jess had gone Dave said, 'There'll be trouble if you start fraternizing with her crowd.'

The word 'fraternizing' was loaded. It was used when referring to hobnobbing with the enemy. Dave had used it deliberately. He liked to be annoying. He wasn't happy with the way things were going for him – Laurie was well aware of that and felt sorry for him – but he could be infuriating!

'Let's go,' she said.

There was no sign of Jess by the time they got out in the street. She'd have been whisked away in her father's car. Laurie and the boys went for the bus. Dave was cheeky to the driver, who threatened to throw him off if he was thinking of causing trouble.

'You and who else?' said Dave.

'Ah, cut it, Dave!' said Barney.

'You're getting to be a dead bore,' Laurie told Dave.

He made a face at her but he did shut up. He gazed moodily out through the bus window. Barney asked about Jess Magowan.

Laurie shrugged. 'I don't really know anything about her.'

'Quite a looker!'

The three of them lived in East Belfast, in a street running off the Newtownards Road. When they got off the bus Laurie saw her mother standing on the opposite pavement, outside Sammy's Fish Bar, where she worked. She was talking to Sammy. She broke away from him to join them as they crossed the road. She was carrying a brown-paper parcel. Fish and chips, for her supper.

'I wish you didn't have to work for a hood like Sammy,' said Laurie.

'Hush your mouth, girl. You know we need the money.'

They turned into their street. Barney said good night to the Magowans at their door and carried on to his own house a few doors up. The houses were the old back-to-backs, sitting straight on to the pavement, and had no gardens, only small yards at the rear where they kept their rubbish bins and the like. Union Jacks flew from several upstairs windows. From a mural on a gable-end wall a hooded gunman with cocked rifle kept watch. The letters UFF were emblazoned beneath. Ulster Freedom Fighters. It was one of a number of outlawed paramilitary organizations, Protestant and Catholic. The UFF was Protestant.

The kerb in front of the Magowans' house had been freshly painted red, white and blue, done by Ed Magowan only that afternoon. He was a firm Loyalist – loyal to the British crown – though had never been a terrorist.

'Your father would be better employed painting the inside of the house!' said Beryl Magowan, unlocking the door.

They went into the living room and Laurie put the kettle on for tea. Her mother sat down in her chip-shop overall to eat her supper. She asked how the evening had gone.

'OK,' said Laurie.

'Dad came by,' said Dave. 'Touched Laurie for a tenner.' He eyed his sister. 'Couldn't pass one this way, could you?'

'Catch yourself on!'

'You could do something about earning your own tenners,' said his mother.

That rattled him. 'Like how?' he demanded. 'Jobs are not exactly lined up on the pavement out there, waiting for me to take my pick.' He hadn't had a job since he'd left school. He was good with cars and he'd have liked to have been an apprentice mechanic, but nobody would give him a chance.

His mother ignored him and asked Laurie, 'So, did you get a good crowd?'

'Very good.' She made the tea and set out the mugs.

'Especially since Uncle Tommy's wee girl was in it,' said Dave.

That got his mother's attention. 'She never was!'

Laurie wasn't going to have said anything to her about Jess Magowan and was furious with Dave for telling her.

'Did you speak to her, Laurie?'

'Speak to her?' said Dave. 'They were all over each other. Kiss, kiss!'

'Why don't you drop dead!'

Laurie poured a mug of tea for herself and took it up to her room. She strummed vigorously on her guitar in an effort to get rid of her annoyance. And she half made up her mind to see Jess again.

A day or two later, Granny Magowan came round. She was going to the bingo with Laurie's mother, who was upstairs getting ready. Granny asked Laurie to play something for her on her guitar.

'Something nice now. None of that Fenian stuff.' Sometimes Laurie played Irish folk music. Her grandmother called it 'Fenian'. She meant Republican.

Laurie played and sang a country song about feeling lonesome that no one could object to.

'Your granda would have enjoyed that, so he would,' said Granny. 'He was great on the flute himself.'

The ould orange flute. They had a picture on the mantelpiece of the old man decked out in his Orange gear, bowler hat, orange sash and all, taken on the twelfth of July. He was stepping out to celebrate the victory of the Battle of the Boyne in 1690, when the armies of the Protestant William of Orange, better known as King Billy, beat the Catholics under the command of James II. Grandpa Magowan had been Grand Master of his Lodge, a man of standing in his community, something his son Ed would never be.

Granny looked up at the picture and sighed. 'Seems like yesterday when that was taken. Time goes fast, so it does.'

'Granny, would you not like to see your son again? Uncle Tommy? I mean, after so long.'

'What's brought him into your head?' Granny's voice was sharp with suspicion.

'Nothing. Just wondered.'

'He chose his life.'

'Just because he married a Catholic?'

'*Just!* It was bad enough him marrying one, but to become one himself! It was a mercy your granda had passed away! It'd have killed him.'

It was at that point that Laurie finally made up her mind. She was going to meet Jess and to hang with the lot of them!

As soon as her mother and grandmother were out of the way, she opened the phone book. She ran her finger down the Magowans until she found a Thomas William at a Holywood address. She dialled. She'd got the right number!

'Laurie!' said Jess. 'I'm dead pleased you've called. I've been hoping you would.'

They arranged to meet downtown on Saturday morning.

On the way Laurie began to have qualms. They might be cousins, related by blood, but that didn't mean they'd have anything more than that in common. And there would be the devil to pay if her father ever found out!

Jess was waiting for her in the café. They settled down with their coffee. Jess asked about Laurie's school, and Laurie asked about Jess's. Jess went to a Catholic school, of course, and Laurie to a Protestant one. There didn't seem a lot of difference between them.

Then they started talking about music and that eased things. Jess said she played the guitar.

'And I sing – a little. Not like you! But I love music.'

'So do I!'

'I could see that! My cousin Neal is great on the fiddle. We like playing together.'

'It must be nice to have someone to play with,' said Laurie. Her friends at school liked listening to music but they weren't interested in making it.

'You could join us for a session sometime if you'd like to.'

Laurie thanked Jess but she didn't commit herself.

She glanced round as the door opened. Two boys and two girls entered in a rush, chatting and laughing.

'What's up?' asked Jess, noticing a change in her cousin's face.

'It's just that boy who's come in –'

'The one who was at your gig?'

'No, not Barney. The other one. We went out together for a year and then he dropped me. Just like that. For her.'

The girl was laughing up into the boy's face. He was smiling. Laurie felt her throat tightening.

'You're as well without him then,' said Jess.

'That's what my mum says.' Laurie tried to smile. 'You going with anyone?'

'Steady, you mean?' Jess laughed. 'No way!'

Barney had caught sight of them and was making his way across.

He said 'Hi!' to them both, but it was Jess he was eyeing. 'We met at the club last Saturday, didn't we?'

'I believe we did.'

'Do you live in the town?'

'No, in Holywood.'

'Holywood, eh? Nice place. I take a run out there from time to time.'

'You don't say!'

'I've got a mountain bike.'

'No mountains in Holywood.'

'It goes on the flat too. Be seeing you.'

He gave them a smile and went back to join his friends.

'He's a great one for the girls,' said Laurie.

'Good-looking, though.'

Barney had an easy manner with him, Laurie admitted. Unlike her own crotchety brother! 'Dave's his own worst enemy, I'm afraid.'

She was surprised at herself talking so openly to someone she scarcely knew. It felt as if they had known each other for much longer.

She opened the magazine she'd bought on the way. 'What star sign are you?'

'Taurus.'

'Me too! When's your birthday?'

'First of May. When's yours?'

'The second!'

'So there's only a day between us. Our mums must have been in hospital at the same time.'

'But different ones.'

They reflected on that for a moment.

'Isn't it crazy,' said Jess, 'this stupid family feud? Keeping it going for ever and ever?'

THREE

Jess and Danny went to school in Belfast. They would normally have gone on the school bus, but their father said he would give them a lift, seeing it was Danny's first morning back. Danny knew he'd be making sure that he actually went!

He made a fuss at breakfast about having a sore stomach – which was true – but that didn't get him anywhere.

'You can't stay at home for the rest of your life,' said his father. 'You've got to keep at your books or you'll not get on in life.' This was one of the sermons he liked to preach to them, especially since he hadn't paid too much attention to books himself.

He dropped them off at the school gate. 'You're not wanting me to come in with you, are you?'

'Certainly not!' Jess slammed the car door shut and took hold of Danny's arm. His body felt draggy. 'Come on, Danny boy!'

She guided him through the heaving mass of bodies in the playground towards the building.

'You'll soon settle down again,' she said. 'You'll see.'

The corridors were quiet. The bell hadn't rung yet. Danny's form teacher was expecting him. She said how pleased she was to see him back and showed him into the classroom, then she came out to have a word with Jess.

'He doesn't want the other kids to know he's got a weak chest,' said Jess. 'He says they'll think he's wet.'

'Mind you, asthma's not uncommon these days.'

Mrs Ryan was sympathetic, though, and said she'd do what she could for him. She couldn't do much in the playground, however. He'd have to make his own friendships. It was unfortunate that his best friend had left a few months ago and gone to live in Omagh.

At break Jess kept an eye on Danny. She followed as he moved down through the crowd towards the edge of the playground.

She saw three boys coming up behind him. They were walking far too close. He was obviously aware of that and quickened his step. They quickened theirs in response. And then the middle one of the three stretched out his foot and tapped Danny on the back of the ankle. Just a neat tap, but enough to make him stumble. He went sprawling into a couple of girls, who rounded on him, asking him what he thought he was doing! The boys doubled up laughing.

Jess cursed them. It didn't take long for bullies to flush out the weak. She'd have liked to have gone and knocked their heads together! But she knew that wouldn't do any good.

At lunchtime she saw the three jerks shadowing Danny again. He ended up standing with his back against the wall.

She waited for him after school. They'd arranged to go along to their father's garage. Danny was mad about cars and would like to be a mechanic when he left school, but Tommy Magowan had other ideas for his son. He wanted him to be a doctor or a lawyer or an accountant. Something respectable so that he could be proud of his son! (That was what Jess said.) She herself was keen on drama and would like to work in the theatre, as a director perhaps, but her father didn't think much of that idea, either. Accountants made more money.

'How did it go?' she asked.

Danny shrugged and she didn't press him.

Neal was in the garage yard, working on a car. Danny asked him what the problem was, and Neal was explaining, when a car drove in at the side gate and a heavy-looking guy with a square head got out.

He took his time coming across to them. He looked Jess and Danny over, then fixed his eye on Neal.

'Can I help you at all?' asked Neal.

'I hear the place has changed hands recently.'

'The new owner's Tommy Magowan. He's not in at the minute, I'm afraid.'

'He's not had a garage round here before, has he?'

'No. He was a manager, down Bangor way.'

Jess studied the tattoos on the back of the man's hands. The Union flag, the Red Hand of Ulster and crossed rifles.

'Give Mr Magowan a message for me, would you?' he said. 'Tell him Sammy called.'

'Sammy?' said Neal.

'Aye,' said Sammy. 'Tell him I'll be back.'

He strolled over to his car, got in, readjusted his mirrors and took up his mobile phone. He drove out with it clamped to his ear and one hand resting casually on the steering wheel.

'Fancies himself,' said Jess.

'Mr Cool,' said Danny.

Tommy Magowan arrived a few minutes later. They told him about the visitor and he called over John, the chief mechanic, who had worked at the garage under the previous owner. Tommy asked him if he knew a man called Sammy.

''Fraid I do,' said John.

'Oh, it's like that, is it?'

'He runs a fish and chip shop on the Newtownards Road, among other things. It's a good front for his other activities.'

'So, what would he be after?'

'Money.'

'You mean protection money?'

'That'd be my guess.'

'Well, he can go jump in the Lough!' said Tommy Magowan, and he went striding off into the building.

John shook his head. 'I hope it's not himself that ends up in the Lough!'

He didn't know his boss too well yet, not the way

his children did. They knew he was good at mouthing off without thinking and then caving in when he came to his senses. At least they hoped he would come to his senses in this case!

'That Sammy guy looked like he really meant business,' said Danny.

'Don't say anything about him to Mum,' warned Jess. 'She'd go up the wall.'

Neal came home with them for supper. He often did. He had his fiddle with him. He and Jess were going to play some music together afterwards.

Danny had been lively enough at the garage but he was gloomy over supper and didn't eat much.

'Is it school that's bothering you, son?' asked his mother.

He gave one of his shrugs. He was into shrugging at present. It saved answering.

'You'll soon make friends again.'

'They've all got their friends.'

'Ah, well,' said his father, 'everybody's got their problems in life.'

Danny made a face at him behind his back.

Jess put the family's problems out of her mind while she and Neal were playing. That was one of the great joys about music, she found: it took your mind off things.

When they stopped for a break she raised the subject of the song-writing competition. She suggested trying to get Laurie to come in with them. Neal was all for the idea, so Jess went straight away to ring her.

★

The three of them met downtown the following evening.

Neal had brought a leaflet about the competition with him. They huddled round it.

CAN YOU WRITE A SONG?
DO YOU PLAY SOLO OR IN A GROUP?
ARE YOU UNDER 18?
HERE'S YOUR CHANCE TO WIN £1,000
SECOND PRIZE £500
THIRD PRIZE £250
ORIGINAL SONGS ONLY
ALL THREE WINNERS TO APPEAR ON TV
SEND A TAPE TO –

It gave the address, a Belfast one, underneath.

'Imagine, the chance to appear on TV!' Jess's dark eyes glowed. In her head she was already there, in the studio, under the brilliant lights.

'Thousands will send in tapes,' said Laurie.

'You know what they say about nothing ventured?' said Jess.

'I do. But where could we do it? You can't sing and play in a café.'

'That's true,' said Neal cheerfully. 'We'd need to find somewhere we could make a racket.'

'But where?' said Laurie again.

They couldn't go to her house, obviously not! Or to Neal's. Or Jess's.

'There's got to be somewhere,' said Jess.

They brooded on it for a while.

'Even coming here wasn't that easy for me,' said

Laurie. 'I had to shake Dave off. Barney told him that he'd seen us together on Saturday.'

'I'll think of something,' said Jess.

After school next day she called in at her mother's dress boutique. She'd got some new tops in. Jess trawled along a rail and pulled out a vivid orange one.

'You can have that if you want,' said her mother. 'It would suit you to wear a strong colour for a change instead of all that black. You look as if you're going to a funeral half the time.'

Jess put the top against herself and squinted in the mirror. 'I don't think it's for me.' She put it back. 'Mum, you're not in favour of carrying on this stupid family feud for ever, are you?'

'Well, no, but –'

'I'm fed up with but! Mum, I might as well tell you – I've been seeing Laurie.'

'Laurie *Magowan*?'

'Well, why shouldn't I? I like her and she's done nothing to us.'

Maeve Magowan sighed. 'I have to agree with you there. But you know your dad wouldn't. Not after the way his family treated him.'

'Told him not to darken their door again!'

'More or less. Said they weren't wanting any Micks in their family! Your dad and his brother even came to blows.'

'Like a couple of kids in the playground!'

'It was a lot more serious than that.'

'I know.' Jess sobered. 'But, anyway, I am going to go on seeing Laurie.'

'Just keep it from your dad, that's all.'

'Neal and I want to have a music session with Laurie. But we need somewhere to play.'

'You can't come to the house!' The very thought of it alarmed Maeve. 'Out of the question!'

'I wasn't thinking of the house! We could practise in the back shop. In the evening, after you've closed. Dad never comes down here in the evening.'

'That would be the one time that he did. The answer's no, Jess! I'm not going to do that behind his back.'

The bell over the door rang and a customer came in. Maeve rose to greet her.

'I've got that dress in for you, Mrs McMordie.'

'Mum?' Jess made one more appeal to her.

'Leave it, Jess!' she said in a tight voice and went into the back shop to fetch Mrs McMordie's dress.

Jess was in a bad mood now, so instead of going on up the hill and home she went down to the shore, which at this part was made up of large, jagged rocks. She perched on one and fired stones through the waves.

'Hi, there!'

She looked round. There was Barney on the path, dismounting from his mountain bike!

'What are you doing here?' she asked.

'Told you I sometimes came out for a run, didn't I? I felt like some fresh air.'

He left his bike on the path and vaulted over the wall. He parked himself on a stone alongside her.

'How about you?' he asked. 'What are you up to?'

'I'm annoyed!'

'Not with me, I hope?'

'No, my mother.'

Jess told Barney her problem. He didn't know somewhere they could practise, did he? No old sheds round his way, no empty garages?

''Fraid not.'

'I'm really fed up with all this Catholic–Protestant nonsense. I mean, it doesn't bother me that you're a Prod.'

'I'm glad to hear it. It doesn't bother me that you're a Mick.'

They laughed.

'It surprises me,' she said, 'that you're not bothered, coming from a street like yours. Orange to a man. And woman.'

'I'm not in the Orange Order. Neither's Dave. He doesn't like marching no more than I do. My auntie's married to a Catholic.'

'Is that a fact?'

'They live in England but they come over and visit. My mum doesn't mind as long as no one knows he's a Catholic.'

They laughed again.

'Our neighbours are Protestant, on either side,' said Jess. 'We've no problems.'

'But that's different, isn't it?'

It was. She lived in a middle-class street that was not so clearly defined.

They listened to the sound of the waves. Jess felt at ease with him.

'It's great getting out the town,' he said. 'I'll need to do it more often.'

FOUR

Barney and Dave were in the living room playing a video game when Laurie came in from school. Barney was winning. He usually did.

Dave jumped up in disgust. 'Ah, stuff it!'

'You don't keep your mind on the game, that's your trouble,' said Barney.

'He's too restless,' said Laurie.

'Wouldn't you be, stuck inside this stupid box all day?'

'You should have stayed on at school, like Barney.'

'I'm glad I'm being held up as an example!' said Barney. He was good at maths and drawing and wanted to be a draughtsman.

'It was driving me nuts,' said Dave. 'You know that.'

'You should go out more during the day,' said Laurie. 'Go up Cave Hill. Get some fresh air.' Why didn't he *do* something? Play football. Go to the swimming baths. Play the tin whistle. Anything!

'It's been raining buckets,' said Dave. 'Maybe you haven't noticed?'

'We could be doing with a week in Florida,' said Barney.

'What's wrong with two weeks?' said Dave.

'Dream on,' said Laurie, and went upstairs to change. She put on clean jeans and a new cornflower-blue top she'd bought the Saturday before. Blue suited her; it emphasized the colour of her eyes. She smeared some blue shadow on her lids.

By the time she went back downstairs, Barney had gone.

'Where are you off to?' asked Dave.

'Nowhere in particular.'

'You're not going to the launderette looking like that, are you? All toshed up.'

'I am not toshed up.' Laurie pulled on her jacket and lifted her guitar from the corner.

'Got a music lesson?'

She didn't answer. She hoped he wasn't going to be a nuisance.

'I'll walk you along the road,' he said.

'You needn't bother.'

'It's no bother. I could even carry your guitar.'

'I can carry my own guitar, thank you.'

'You're your own woman, aren't you, Laurie?'

'Oh, belt up!'

He followed her out. She set briskly off towards the river. He walked a pace or two behind her, whistling an Orange marching tune and putting her teeth on edge.

Before she reached Albert Bridge she stopped and

wheeled round to face him. 'What do you think you're doing?'

'You're always telling me I should get more fresh air.'

'Well, turn right around and get it in the opposite direction!' She stole a quick look at her watch. She'd be late for the train if she hung about too long.

'Got a date, have you? Don't worry, I won't cramp your style.'

'Why don't you get lost! Like I mean, permanently.'

'That's not a very Christian thing to say.'

Laurie walked on, since there was nothing much else she could do. She wished she could throw him over the bridge, but he was heavier than she was! She halted again outside the entrance of Central Station.

'You don't want to miss your train, do you?' said Dave. 'You are going to Holywood, aren't you?'

'Were you listening to my phone call?'

He grinned.

She turned into the station. The only hope now was to ignore him. Freeze him off. And with luck he wouldn't have enough money for the fare. Luck wasn't with her that evening. Dave slid into the queue behind her and bought a ticket for Holywood.

She got into the first carriage, he followed. He sat a couple of rows further back and resumed his whistling.

He rose when she did. The train took only ten minutes to Holywood.

'I'm warning you, Dave Magowan!' she said as they stood waiting for the train to come to a full stop.

'I'm just wanting to make sure our Fenian relatives don't steal you.'

She jumped off the moment the door opened. Dave looked back along the platform.

'Friend of yours?' he said.

She glanced round to see Neal emerging from the carriage behind theirs. She didn't wait for him to catch up but carried on along the path down on to the roadway and then through the subway. It was gloomy and it smelled. There was no one else about. Their feet echoed in the hollow.

'Girl like you shouldn't be out alone in a place like this,' said Dave. 'Just as well I came.'

Laurie walked faster. He did too.

Jess was waiting as arranged at the top of the underpass. She had her guitar with her as well. She looked dumbfounded when she saw Dave sloping along beside Laurie.

'Don't worry, I didn't ask him!' said Laurie. 'He's not going to join us for the evening.'

'Just fancied a night out in Holywood,' said Dave. 'Bright lights and all that.'

Holywood had a couple of main shopping streets and a lot of leafy suburban roads.

Neal came up the slope and joined them. He was carrying his fiddle.

'Are you going busking, the three of you?' said Dave. 'That could be a real gas. I could collect the money.'

They ignored him. Jess led the way up into the town. Dave lagged a few yards behind.

'Will he tell on you, Laurie?' asked Jess.

Laurie didn't think so. 'He's a pain in the neck but he's not a grass.'

'Are we going to your house, Jess?' asked Neal.

'No! Wait and see!'

There weren't many people about. Jess halted at the entrance to a lane. 'Better tell Dave not to follow us any further, Laurie.'

'OK, Dave!' said Laurie. 'It's this far and no further. I'll kill you if you come another inch.'

'I'm too young to die!' He clutched his throat. 'I'll keep guard here for you but.'

'Just don't attract attention, that's all!'

They turned into the lane and Jess stopped at a dark-green door. 'Maeve Magowan' was printed above the bell.

'Does your mum know?' asked Neal.

'Certainly not! She'd be furious if she found out. She won't, though. She's gone to the pictures. I talked Dad into taking her.'

Jess fished a key out of her pocket and unlocked the door.

'Can you see? I'll put the light on after I get the blinds down.'

Once they were inside and the light was on Laurie saw that they were in a back shop. There were boxes piled up and blouses hung on a rail. The place smelled of fresh new clothes.

'It's my mum's shop,' said Jess. 'If we stay at the back nobody will know we're here.'

She locked the door and made sure the blinds were down tight, then she switched on an electric fire. 'We might as well be comfortable.'

They tuned their instruments and since Laurie was ready first Jess suggested she made some coffee. There was a jar on the draining board and a kettle. Laurie made three mugs of coffee. She liked the cosy feel of the place, with the night and everybody they knew shut out. Dave shut out. She hoped his feet were freezing into boards out there!

Dave leaned against the shop's plate-glass window, his collar pulled up against the wind. He was beginning to think better of this lark.

Hearing the sound of roller blades, he looked round and saw a boy bearing down the pavement towards him. He had a bag of chips in his hands which he was eating while he rolled. The smell of the chips reached Dave, making him feel hungry.

The boy did a fancy twirl and came to a halt in front of him.

'Are you looking for something?'

'What's it to you?' Dave straightened himself up. The kid was almost as tall as he was, but skinny, and younger.

'Just wondered. That's my mum's shop.'

'Well, well! You must be Danny boy! I've heard tell of you.'

'So who are you?'

'Your cousin Dave.'

'You're joking!'

'I never joke.'

'Have a chip,' said Danny. 'Help yourself.'

Dave took a handful. 'So you like roller-blading?'

'Yeah. Do you?'

'It's OK. I prefer cars.'

'Who wouldn't!'

'I like speed. Speed's great. It blows the mind, so it does!'

'I know what you mean. I can't wait to drive.'

'Hasn't your dad ever let you have a go? And him with a garage?'

'No chance! Have you a licence, Dave?'

Dave shrugged.

'You've driven but, have you?' said Danny.

'I might have.'

'So what are you doing out this way?' asked Danny.

'I'm keeping guard. Our sisters are in there.' Dave jerked his thumb at the window. 'Can you hear?'

The musicians were enjoying themselves. They were managing to get a bit of a tune going – not a great one perhaps, but it was a start.

'We should try to make up some words,' said Jess.

'What could they be about?' said Laurie.

'Love?' suggested Neal.

'There are far too many songs about love,' said Jess. 'Unrequited love. I'm sick of people wailing on about being dumped.' She added quickly, with a glance at Laurie, 'My big mouth! I didn't mean you, Laurie.'

'It's OK!'

Neal gave Laurie a curious look but he didn't say anything.

Laurie agreed with what Jess had said, though. She'd been singing a few songs of that kind recently and they hadn't done much to cheer her up. She'd had to shake herself out of it. 'What about friendship?' she said.

'We could write about us!' Jess thought for a moment, then said melodramatically, 'You are my friend for evermore!'

They giggled at that.

'Go on, Laurie,' said Neal. 'Give it a go. "You are my friend for evermore."'

Laurie sang and they played along, then she sang the line again, beginning to get a feel for it.

'Bravo!' cried Neal, waving his bow in the air. 'Now what?'

'Though our families fight their war,' said Jess tentatively. 'Try that, Laurie.'

She tried it. It sounded not too bad.

'Let's have the two lines together now!' said Neal.

They were getting carried away and making so much noise that they almost didn't hear the knocking on the door. They quietened to listen. If it was Dave, Laurie was determined to strangle him!

'Open up!' a voice shouted on the other side of the door. 'Police!'

FIVE

The police were in the middle of interrogating them – and that was what it felt like, being interrogated, rather than questioned – when the door opened and in walked Tommy and Maeve Magowan.

'Dad!' gasped Jess.

The Magowans had seen the police car parked outside and the lights on and had naturally been interested.

By this time everyone was in the front shop, since the back had been too crowded with seven people in it. The police had picked up Danny and Dave on the way and brought them in. Danny was still wearing his roller blades and he smelt of chips.

There wasn't too much room in the front shop either, between the rails of garments and the counter and the cheval mirror.

'What's going on here?' demanded Tommy Magowan, his eyes out on stalks. Jess hoped he wouldn't have a heart attack.

'I thought you were at the pictures?' she said.

'The pictures were rubbish! I wasn't going to waste

my time on stuff like that.' He turned to the two constables. 'Has there been a break-in?'

'We're not sure, sir. These two lads were loitering about outside.' The constable indicated Danny and Dave, who were trying to get lost behind a rail of satin evening tops. 'When they saw us they nipped off down the lane pretty smart. So we followed and came on in and found these other three through the back. The girl here says she's your daughter. We'd like you to confirm that.'

Jess's father now confronted her. She could see that he would have liked to deny it. She could almost hear his voice ringing out, 'She's no daughter of mine!' Instead he said grimly, 'She's my daughter all right.' He looked across at Danny's head just visible above cerise satin. 'And he is my son. And this is my nephew, Neal O'Shea, who works in my garage. I am not acquainted with the other two.' He was having a job to control himself.

'We'll be getting along,' said Dave, sliding out from behind the rail.

'Oh, no, you won't,' said the constable, taking hold of his arm. Unfortunately for Dave, he looked like the kind of boy that the police pick up at the slightest excuse.

Jess swallowed hard. 'Dad, this is Laurie Magowan, your brother Ed's daughter. We were just playing some music together. And this is her brother, Dave.'

The constables looked questioningly at Tommy, awaiting confirmation of this also. His Adam's apple was jerking up and down.

'He can't actually confirm it,' said Jess, 'because he's

never seen them before. You see, he hasn't set eyes on his brother –'

'I don't think you need to go into our family history, Jess,' said her mother, who until then had been standing in the background, trying to catch her eye so that she could glare at her. 'I think, officers, that you can take my daughter's word for it. And we needn't detain you any longer. I expect you've other work to do. I'm sorry you've been troubled.'

The policemen left. There was silence in the shop.

'We weren't doing any harm, Dad,' said Jess. 'We were only making music.' What could be more innocent than that? They hadn't been rumbling about the streets, disturbing the peace.

'You'd no business being in here at all at this time of night. We wouldn't have been covered for insurance if you'd burned the place down.' As if that was his real objection!

'We haven't been lighting fires!' protested Jess.

'We've been very careful, Uncle Tommy,' said Neal.

'I'm surprised at you being part of this, Neal,' said Tommy, and Neal coloured. Jess felt sorry for him, as she knew her father thought him a responsible lad, which he was on the whole. But no one could be responsible all the time, at least not while they were young. That was what she always told her mother anyway.

'Dad, it was all my idea,' she said.

'I'll bet it was!'

'Laurie and Dave will have to be getting home. They've got to catch a train back to Belfast.'

Dave disappeared into the back in a flash. Laurie hesitated before saying goodbye to the room in general.

'Cheerio, Laurie,' said Neal. 'See you soon.'

Jess followed Laurie and Dave through to the back shop.

'What a scene!' said Dave, grinning.

'I'm sorry, Jess,' said Laurie. 'Will you be all right?'

'Of course! He's not going to beat me up!'

Jess opened the door and let them out.

Laurie rounded on Dave as soon as the door closed behind them.

'That was all your fault!'

'How was it?'

'I told you not to attract attention! You cause trouble wherever you go.'

'Danny and I were standing there minding our own business when this police car pulls up. Could I help it?'

'You shouldn't have been there in the first place.'

They went along the lane and turned into the street.

A Jaguar was parked at the kerb, a brand-new one, judging from the licence plate. Dave stopped to admire it.

'Would that be Uncle Tommy's, do you think? Hey, did you get a load of our uncle?' Dave put on a mimicking voice. '"I'm not acquainted with those two scum and I'm not wanting to be."' He let his hand trail over the Jaguar's bonnet. 'I could go for a car like this.'

'Don't you dare, Dave Magowan!' warned Laurie.

★

Jess wasn't frightened of her father in the way that she sensed Laurie and Dave might be of theirs. Laurie had hinted that his temper was vile when he'd been drinking. His brother Tommy drank only moderately and his bark was definitely a great deal worse than his bite. There wasn't much he could do in this instance except bark, Jess knew, and perhaps cut her pocket money, which was what he did when they got home.

'If you can't behave in a responsible way then you don't deserve to have an allowance. And what is more, you are *not* to see those two again. I forbid you to! Understand?'

Jess went up to Danny's room after her father had finished his tirade.

'What did you make of Dave?' she asked.

'Thought he was OK,' said Danny casually.

'You don't want to have anything to do with him! He's trouble, from what I hear.'

'He's into cars,' said Danny, as if that excused everything.

Jess gave her brother a thoughtful look before going off to her own room. She lay for a long time unable to sleep while she turned these new problems over in her mind. She wasn't too worried about the allowance – she had some money in the post office that she'd been saving for a new CD player which she could use until her father softened up, which he would, given time. She was more bothered about finding a new venue for their rehearsals. She had a few wild ideas, like taking refuge in a wood or going up Cave Hill, but that would be cold on the feet, let alone the hands. A garage would be ideal. Her father's was obviously out of the question. It was locked up like a fortress at night anyway. And there was always the chance of running into Sammy.

Sammy came back to the garage next day.

When Neal and Tommy came in in the morning they found that two cars had been badly scraped and dented along their sides. It looked as if someone had taken the claw end of a hammer to them. One car was going to need a new door. John was sure it would have been the work of Sammy's men. 'Just a gentle opening shot. A nudge like.' He knew Sammy's ways.

'I'd like to nudge him into the middle of next week!' declared Tommy, frowning and scratching the bald patch on the back of his head.

While they were examining the cars, the man in question turned up.

'Boys a dear, those are bad scratches you've got there!' said he. 'Will you be able to mend them, do you think, Mr Magowan? I take it you are Mr Magowan, the proprietor of this garage? Maybe I could be of some service to you?'

'In what way like?' said Tommy, his voice heavy on the sarcasm. 'Put on armed guards?'

'That wouldn't be necessary. Not if it was known I was looking after the place.'

'They'd lay off?'

'You're fast on the uptake!' said Sammy with a smile. Then he dropped it and said, 'People don't mess with Sammy, you can take my word for that.'

'How about the police?'

'Is that a threat, Mr Magowan?' The smile was back again. 'The police are far too busy to fuss over two scratched cars. Think it over. But don't take too long thinking. I'm not known for my patience.'

'Your dad will have to give in,' said Neal, when he told Jess about it later. 'It seems nobody gets the better of Sammy.'

Jess wasn't surprised her father was in a bad temper these days. He'd had enough with the fiasco in the shop and now he had a Mafia-type hood on his back. She stayed out of his way as much as possible.

She met Barney again down by the shore, this time by arrangement. Her father never went for walks, so she wasn't worried about bumping into him. She couldn't tell him she was seeing Barney. A friend of Dave's, living in the same street!

'I'm in everybody's bad books,' she said mournfully to Barney.

'Except mine,' he said, slipping his arm round her waist.

She leaned against him. He had a solid, comfortable feel to him. It was getting dark and the lights were coming on across the Lough, in Carrickfergus and Whitehead and Greenisland.

'I like this time of night,' she said.

'So do I!' he said.

He kissed her.

'I liked that,' he said.

'So did I,' she said, and so he kissed her again.

They stayed down on the rocks for a long time, and when she got in and her father asked her where she had been she said that she had gone for a walk.

'In the dark?' he said. 'By yourself?'

'I was quite safe,' she said.

SIX

Dave was at a loose end. He called on Barney, but Barney was busy.

'I've got work to do, man,' he said.

'Homework,' said Dave with disgust.

Barney shrugged.

'See you, I guess, one of these days,' said Dave, and drifted off down the street.

He was getting fed up with Barney. If he wasn't doing his homework he was seeing that blasted Fenian cousin of his. Bitch! Didn't Barney realize he was running a risk seeing her? Lots of people wouldn't like it. Barney's dad wouldn't. He'd go ape. Or was Barney so gone on Miss Fancy Pants that he didn't care? But he never stuck long with a girl. Dave comforted himself with that thought and took a swipe with his foot at a loose stone laying on the pavement.

Near the corner he bumped into Sammy, almost literally. He hadn't been looking where he was going.

'Whoa there, Dave!' Sammy took hold of his shoulders and kept hold of them for a few seconds before releasing him. 'You're the very lad I was wanting to see.'

Dave shuffled his feet and thought of escape, but nobody got away from Sammy until he was willing to let them go.

'You seem to have a lot of time on your hands these days?' said Sammy.

Dave grunted.

'Maybe I could find a wee job for you?'

'In the chip shop like?' said Dave. He wouldn't fancy coming home smelling of frying every night like his mum. No way!

'No, I wasn't thinking of that. This wouldn't take too much of your time. Just an hour or so round lunchtime, and in the afternoon, when the school's coming out.'

'Oh, no, I don't think –' said Dave, and he hurriedly began trying to back away. He ended up jarring his left shoulder against the wall.

'Maybe you should think. It'd be easy-peasy for you. You'd know a lot of the kids.' Sammy rummaged in his pocket. 'Here, son, I've a wee thing here for you. Give us your hand!'

Dave hesitated, then did as he was told. Sammy covered Dave's hand with his own and dropped something into it. Dave gazed down at his palm. In the hollow lay a small packet.

'I'll be in touch,' said Sammy, and away he went round the corner and out of sight.

Dave was sweating. He leaned back against the wall. He was still gazing at the packet, so he didn't see that his sister was standing only a few yards from him.

She came up to him.
'What did Sammy give you?'
'Nothing.' He closed his hand into a tight fist.
'Yes, he did! I saw him.' Laurie seized Dave's wrist. Her grip was surprisingly strong. He'd never known her so fierce before. 'Show me!'
'Lay off!'
'I won't, unless you let me see!'
'OK then, see!'
He uncurled his hand to show the packet.
'What's in there?'
'I don't know.'
'Well, look!'
He shook six small white tablets into the palm of his other hand. They gazed down at them.
'Throw them away!' said Laurie.
'I will! I can't drop them here on the pavement but, can I? Some kid might pick them up.'
'Why did he give them to you?'
'I don't know.'
'Don't give me that! Was he wanting you to push for him?'
'He said it was a present.'
'Sammy doesn't give presents.'
'Anyway, I wouldn't push.'
'You'd better not! Dad'd skin the hide off you.'
'Look, Laurie, I'm not wanting to get mixed up with Sammy. What do you take me for? I know he's bad news.'
'He's more than bad news. He's evil.'
'OK, OK, don't keep going on!' Dave slid the tablets back into the packet and put it in his pocket.

'I'll get rid of them, honest. Where are you off to?'

'To see a friend.'

'Wouldn't be Cousin Jess, would it?'

'None of your business,' said Laurie. He would have an orange fit if he knew *where* she was going. She was not feeling too calm about it herself.

'I suppose you couldn't lend us a couple of quid, could you?'

She groaned but gave it to him. He didn't have much going for him, after all. That was what she told herself every time she gave in to him. There had to come a time when she didn't give in! He'd have to do something to sort himself out. But what?

'Ta, Laurie. Don't know what I'd do without you. See you!'

She watched him nip across the main road, dodging a car. She waited. She wanted to make sure he didn't follow her. On the opposite pavement he stopped to speak to a couple of boys called Gregg and Jamieson, well known in the area as troublemakers. They were bad news and all! Dave had taken up with them recently, now that he didn't have Barney to go about with so much.

They disappeared down a side street and Laurie carried on towards town. Jess was waiting for her with her guitar at the end of Albert Bridge.

'You didn't bring your guitar, Laurie?'

'I wasn't wanting to rouse Dave's suspicions.'

'Not nervous, are you?'

'A bit.'

'Don't worry. You have me with you. Just stick close. You won't have to speak to anyone.'

They crossed the road and entered the Republican Short Strand. It was only a short distance from where Laurie lived but she'd only ever skirted the edge. She'd never been into the heart of it. It felt like alien territory. Enemy territory, that's what Dave would have called it.

Her eyes were immediately taken by the IRA graffiti and murals. One large mural covered a whole wall with people's faces and the words: THIS MURAL IS DEDICATED TO *ALL* THOSE FROM THIS AREA WHO DIED IN BRITAIN'S WAR IN IRELAND. Another wall was decorated with two hooded gunmen. Laurie studied the murals under lowered eyelids, unable to bring herself to look at them straight on.

'You've got your own graffiti,' said Jess.

'Oh, yes!' Laurie couldn't deny that. They had 'Ulster's Freedom Corner' near them, which was a whole set of murals, a shrine to the Loyalist cause. This sort of political graffiti was being claimed by some as part of their cultural heritage!

They passed a police station, grilled and barred like a fortress, the way all the police stations were in the province. Laurie had been amazed when she'd visited an aunt on the mainland to find that you could walk right into a police station without being challenged.

They turned into another street. A woman was coming along the pavement towards them. Jess gave a start.

'Jess!' said the woman.

'Aunt Maureen!' said Jess.

'I didn't know you were coming here the night. Neal's not in, I'm afraid.'

'Oh, he's not?' said Jess lamely, knowing full well that he would not be. 'Aunt Maureen, this is Laura.'

'Hello, Laura.' Neal's mother gave her a direct look. 'You one of Jess's school pals?'

'Just a pal,' said Jess hastily.

'Well, I must be going. Nice meeting you, Laura.'

'Nice meeting you, Mrs O'Shea,' said Laurie.

Neal's mother walked on.

'I hope you didn't mind me calling you Laura!' said Jess. 'I was just wanting to disguise you a bit.'

'Call me anything you like!'

'Aunt Maureen's had a hard time. Her husband – my mum's brother – got killed in a pub bombing.'

Planted there by one of her lot, Laurie presumed. Not that they were actually 'her lot', just because they were Protestant. Far from it.

'Poor Neal,' she said.

They stopped at a garage and Jess gave three short taps and two long ones on the door. It was opened by Neal.

'Come on in!'

A dangling bulb cast a weak glow over the place. There was nothing in it except for a few old tyres and cans.

'Are you allowed to be in here?' asked Laurie. She had visions of another police raid and having to give her address. And then would come the question, 'So what's someone like you doing in these parts?'

'Don't worry,' said Neal, 'it's all legal! The owner hasn't got a car, so he lets me use it to do odd jobs for people round about. He said it was fine by him if I wanted to practise the fiddle in here.'

Neal fastened the door securely and they began their session. Jess had been working on the next two lines of their song, so now they had a verse!

'You are my friend for evermore
Though our families fight their war.
Try to forget and put past what is gone
Trust and unite in our song.'

'Wouldn't it be great if we could get our fathers to unite in song!' said Jess.

'Fat chance!' said Laurie.

After their rehearsal Neal walked them to the edge of the Short Strand. Laurie felt more comfortable with him escorting them, though she still couldn't help glancing over her shoulder.

They arranged another meeting, then the girls left Neal and crossed over.

'He's easy to be with, isn't he?' said Laurie. 'Easy to talk to.'

Jess wondered if Laurie would be interested in Neal. She knew he was taken by her. He'd told her so. She'd said another O'Shea tangling with another Magowan would create another furore in the family! He'd shrugged and said times had changed. For some people, maybe. But not their families. They put up the barricades the minute they heard the word 'change'. You'd have thought their heads were set in concrete! Her father had made a big change in his life when he'd married her mother, but it was as if, having done that, he'd decided enough was enough, and the way he was then was the way he would stay for life.

The girls were having a last chat on the corner before parting when Laurie heard herself being hailed in a loud, drunken voice. Dave hove into sight, accompanied by two of his mates.

'Dave!' she cried. 'You've been drinking!'

'I've always told you she was a smart girl, haven't I?' he said to his companions. 'She catches on quick. And I see you've got Cousin Jess with you, after all. Hello, Cousin Jess. Whatcha doin' slummin' down our way?'

'Cut it, Dave,' said Laurie.

'Is she your cousin?' said one of them. 'Not a bad-looking bird.'

Jess would have liked to clout him with her guitar but she didn't want to run the risk breaking it over his head. She was waiting for Dave to say she was their Fenian cousin, but it seemed he wasn't that far gone, even with his head stupid with drink.

'So that's what you spent my money on!' said Laurie. 'That's the last I'll ever give you.'

'I've a pound left still.' Dave produced it from his pocket. Then he dropped it and tried to pick it up, but failed. Jess trapped it under her foot.

'See that!' said one of the louts. 'That was fancy footwork!'

'How did you get all that drink then?' Laurie demanded of Dave.

'There's ways and means,' said the other lout with a smirk, answering for him. 'Means and ways.'

Jess said she must be going or she'd miss her train.

'I'll leave you to the station,' said the smirker.

'No, thanks all the same. I can go on my own. I'll see you, Laurie.'

Jess left them and walked smartly over the bridge towards the station.

'Are you coming, Dave?' asked Laurie.

'Naw. See you later.'

But he came in only ten minutes after her.

She asked him how he'd got the beer. 'Did you steal it?'

'I did not!'

Laurie put the kettle on and spooned coffee into a mug. 'You'd better sober up before Mum comes in.'

He staggered off to the loo. He'd left his jacket hanging on the back of a chair. She didn't like snooping, but sometimes he left her no choice. She slipped her hand into the pockets and pulled out two ten-pound notes.

She was holding them when he came back in. His face was chalk white. He'd been sick.

'What are you doing in my pockets?' he cried. 'You'd no business.'

'Where did you get these?'

'What do you think you are – a bloody cop?'

'Tell me where you got them or I'll show them to Dad.'

'I found them in the gutter.'

He closed in on her. They wrestled. He had her arm twisted round behind her back and the pain was so excruciating that she was on the point of letting go of the money when the door opened and in came their father.

'What the hell do you think you're doing to your sister?'

Dave dropped her arm and she slid the notes into her jeans' pocket.

'It was just a game,' muttered Dave.

'It didn't look like no game to me. She looked like you were hurting her. Are you all right, Laurie?'

'Yes, fine.'

'Don't let me see you doing that to your sister again, do you hear?' Their father raised his hand threateningly to Dave. 'You'll be sorry if you do, I'm warning you.'

SEVEN

When Jess arrived home and was asked the usual question she said she'd been playing music in a garage in the Short Strand with Neal. It was nothing but the truth. It was easy at times to tell the truth, and yet lie. Her father looked suspicious but let it go, saying she'd better get her homework done.

She was finishing it in the playground next morning at break when her friend Bernadette interrupted to say that Danny was in trouble. Jess jumped up, dropping her maths jotter face down in some dirt. Muttering strong words, she gathered her clobber together and followed Bernadette.

Danny was up against the wall with the three bully boys from his class facing him. The girls kept their distance to see what was happening.

Danny had a bag of crisps in his hand and it was this that seemed to be the centre of attention.

'Give us a crisp, Stinge!' cried one of the boys, and reaching out his hand, he snatched the bag. Danny stood as if paralysed.

The boy rammed crisps into his mouth until it was stuffed full. Then he tossed the bag to the next boy, who caught it.

'Yum, yum, salt and vinegar, our favourites! Pass the parcel! Catch!' The third boy caught it.

They gobbled the crisps, throwing some up into the air and catching them in their open, gaping mouths. They then flicked the bag back to Danny. Even from a distance the girls could see that it was empty. Danny looked inside, and squashed it flat.

'We've eaten all Stinge's crisps! What a shame! Boo! Hoo!' They pretended to cry.

Bernadette put a hand on Jess's arm, restraining her. 'Leave it, Jess! Don't interfere. You'll just make it worse for him.'

Bernadette was right.

Jess decided, though, that it was time to have a word with Danny's form teacher.

Mrs Ryan said Jess had been wise not to let the bullying go on any longer. 'I'll have a word with the boys. They're trouble, those three.'

The following afternoon, coming out of school with Bernadette, Jess looked about as usual for Danny. For a moment she couldn't see him. Then Bernadette spotted a knot of boys gathered by the gate.

'Isn't that Danny in amongst them?'

Jess raced down towards the gate, followed by Bernadette. Danny was surrounded. Jess could just make out the top of his head. She heard the words 'snitch' and 'informer'. 'Informer' had a horrible ring to it in their province. Out of breath, she reached the edge of the group.

A boy – older than Danny, whose name she knew to be Riley – was saying to him, 'Do you know what happens to informers, Snitch?' Danny was holding himself as rigid as a stair rod, his hands by his sides. 'Well, maybe you're going to find out!'

Jess went barging into the middle of the circle, shoving a couple of boys aside. 'He's not an informer!' she cried.

'Oh, he's not, is he?' said Riley. 'And did he not go and tell Mrs Ryan he got his crisps pinched? His salt and vinegar crisps. I like cheese and onion myself.'

Thought he was a comedian, did he? His audience was sniggering. The three bully boys were in the front row and enjoying themselves hugely. One was laughing all over his face. Jess longed to push it in. He looked like a younger version of Riley.

'He didn't tell Mrs Ryan,' she said. 'I did.'

'And who are you when you're at home?'

'I'm his sister.'

'His sister, eh? So it was you that grassed on my wee brother?'

Riley came lunging towards her. He was half a head taller, and broader. She saw Danny move, trying to cut him off. And then everyone was flailing about as another body entered the ring.

Jess had arranged to meet Barney further up the road, well away from the school. He had a brown belt at judo. He took hold of Jess's assailant now and flung him back against the railings in one easy movement. The boy stayed there, winded. The others moved back a few feet.

'What's going on here?'

On to the scene came Mr Duggan, who taught English.

'Now then, I want to know what the fighting's about!' He looked over at the railings. 'Are you all right, Riley?'

Riley heaved himself up on to his feet. 'He near broke my back, sir.' He pointed at Barney.

Jess's temper flared. 'It wasn't his fault!'

'He shouldn't be here at all,' said Riley. 'He's not from our school, Mr Duggan.'

'I can see that.'

The whole world could see it just by looking at Barney's school scarf.

'So what's he doing here?' demanded Riley.

'He started the fight, so he did, sir,' said his younger brother.

'That's not true!' Bernadette came forward. 'They were bullying Danny!'

'And they were going to jump on me too,' said Jess. 'Barney here came in to protect me.'

'Is that true?' Mr Duggan turned his attention to the younger Riley.

'Well, sir . . .'

'Look at me when I speak to you. Is it true?'

'We never touched Danny but. We just sort of . . .' His voice trailed off.

'Who else was in on this?'

The younger Riley looked at his two friends and they shuffled unwillingly forward.

'You know we don't tolerate bullying in this school! Go to my room and wait for me there! You too, Riley!' Mr Duggan said to the brother.

They went, with Riley the elder giving Jess a filthy look behind Mr Duggan's back and mouthing a few silent obscenities.

'Sorry about all this,' Mr Duggan said to Barney. 'It won't have given you a very good impression of our school.'

'That's all right. It could have happened just as easily in our school.'

Jess couldn't help smiling. Barney was good at knowing the right thing to say.

'And how about you, Danny?' asked Mr Duggan. 'Are you OK?'

'Fine,' muttered Danny.

'Any more trouble, just you come to me and I'll sort them out. Right?'

Danny nodded.

Mr Duggan went off.

'He's nice, isn't he, Danny?' said Jess. He was her favourite teacher and English was her favourite subject.

'As if I could go to him and tell on them!'

Jess had no answer to that. No one wanted to be known as a grass.

'Let's go!' she said, leading the way out through the gate, walking fast. She wanted to get Barney out of there as quickly as possible.

'You were nuts, you know!' she told him. 'A Prod coming in here like that and laying about you!' She did, however, admire him for doing it.

'I could hardly stand there and watch that lout knocking you about.'

'What did you have to interfere for in the first

place?' Danny rounded on his sister. 'I could have taken care of myself.'

'Sure you could!'

'You don't think I can do anything, do you, any of you?'

With that, Danny spun around and made off in the opposite direction.

'Let him go,' said Barney. 'He's thirteen. He's right – he's got to be able to look after himself. Maybe you have been mollycoddling him a bit too much.'

'For goodness' sake!' Jess exploded. 'I've just been trying to help him. If I hadn't interfered Riley would have beaten him up.'

'I can understand Danny, though. No guy likes his sister having to defend him.'

'Oh, you guys have got your pride, haven't you?' She stormed on ahead of Barney, no longer full of so much admiration for him.

He caught her up and took hold of her hand. 'I know you want to help him. I might be able to as well. I could teach him judo.'

She melted. 'Would you, Barney? That'd be great.'

'No bother.'

But where could he do it? It was back to the old problem again.

'I couldn't really ask you to my house. Too dodgy. You'd get cross-questioned by my dad. It's his speciality. Hey, what about Neal's garage?' Barney knew about their rehearsal arrangements. She'd got into the habit of telling him most things she got up to.

'Go into the Short Strand?' he said indignantly. 'No way!'

EIGHT

Laurie confronted Dave when she came in from school that afternoon.

'What happened to the tablets Sammy gave you?'

'I threw them away.'

'Liar! You sold them, didn't you? *Didn't* you?'

'So what if I did?'

'You told me you wouldn't push drugs!'

'That wasn't pushing. I wasn't talking anybody into it. He was a druggie already.'

'What did you get for them?'

'Forty quid.'

'You're a fool, Dave Magowan!'

'Quit the slagging, will you! I'm not going to start pushing, I tell you! Honest I'm not.'

'Stay away from Gregg and Jamieson then!'

But would they stay away from him? That was the problem. And what about Sammy? Laurie knew it was unlikely the drugs had been a free gift. Sammy extorted a price for everything.

'Where's my twenty quid?' asked Dave.

'Down a grating. I tore it up and shoved it down.'

'You did *what*?'

'You heard.'

'It was *my* money!'

'It wasn't yours at all. It was dirty money.'

'You'd no right doing that!'

'I'd every right.'

Laurie turned and walked back out of the house. It was raining slightly but she didn't care. She needed air. Her head felt fuddled. The light beads of rain were refreshing on her face.

What could she do about Dave!

She was heading up the main road when a bicycle bell shrilled behind her, cutting into her thoughts.

'Hi, Laurie!' It was Neal, on his way home from work. 'You look a bit damp! Fancy a coffee somewhere?'

She did.

He pushed his bike and they went to a café well away from his district, or hers. She told him about Dave.

'He needs a job to turn him around.'

'Pity he can't work for us,' said Neal.

That wasn't on, of course. And the only other garage where Neal had contacts was owned by a Catholic. He thought they might be looking for a trainee mechanic but neither Dave nor his father would go for that! Yet in Tommy Magowan's garage Catholics and Protestants worked happily side by side, from what Neal said. The others were all Protestant apart from himself and his uncle.

They drank their coffee and had another, and a

toasted cheese sandwich to go with it, and then Neal asked Laurie if she'd feel like going to the pictures. She said that she would. One thing she didn't feel like was going home.

'I've no money on me, but.'

'That's all right. It'll be my treat.'

They went to the Strand Cinema, further up the road. Neal bought a bag of popcorn and two cans of Coke. It was a relief for Laurie to be able to sit companionably with him in the warm dark and forget about family problems for a while.

Afterwards, emerging into the street, he tried to take her hand, but she pulled it away.

'Sorry!' He dropped his hand as if it had been burned.

'Neal,' she said, embarrassed. 'I like you a lot, I really do, but I'm not wanting to get involved in anything. You see, I've not long broken up with my last boyfriend. I'd just like us to be friends.'

'That's fine,' he said, but from the tone of his voice Laurie knew he was hurt. She didn't want to hurt him but she couldn't lead him up the garden path either.

He didn't say much on the way home and long before they reached Laurie's street she said that he should go on ahead.

'I wouldn't want you to run into Dave and his friends.'

'Are you sure?'

She nodded.

'See you then.' He jumped on his bike and took off as if he was relieved to get away.

Now Laurie felt down again. These swings of mood

were getting to her! She phoned Jess when she got in. They had a chat most evenings.

'Neal might not want me to be in the song competition with you now.'

'He's not one to hold a grudge,' said Jess. 'Once he gets over his disappointment he'll be fine.'

Neal was such a decent guy, Laurie reflected, when she was lying awake in bed, that it was a pity she couldn't have him for a boyfriend. You'd always know you could trust him. But he *was* a Catholic and that would hold her back. It wasn't that she was prejudiced against Catholics but she thought it would cause problems in a relationship in the long run, certainly if it came to marrying and having kids. Uncle Tommy had solved it by turning, but she could never see herself doing that.

A couple of days later, they had another rehearsal. Neal showed no signs of holding a grudge against her, though there was some tension between them.

In the middle of the session there came a knock on the door. They stopped playing. They looked at one another. The knock repeated itself. Not the police again, surely not!

'Who is it?' asked Neal.

'Grandpa. That's you, isn't it, Neal? I could hear you playing. Can I come in?'

''Fraid not, Grandpa, not right now.'

'Why not? Have you a girl in there?' He rattled the door handle.

The girls started to giggle and couldn't stop. Neal was looking flustered, which he didn't often do.

'Do you hear me, Neal?' demanded Grandpa O' Shea.

'I hear you but I'm busy.'

That set them off afresh. Soon their sides were aching and their eyes streaming. Grandpa O'Shea's feet shuffled off, accompanied by the slow tap of his stick.

Now Neal could see the funny side too. He joined in their laughter and the tension between him and Laurie evaporated.

They sobered and took up their instruments again.

'You've got a great voice, Laurie,' said Jess as they were packing up afterwards. 'You really should take up singing professionally when you leave school.'

'How could I do that?'

'Go to college. Study music.'

'I'd love to.'

'Do it then!' said Neal. He had wanted to go to college himself to study engineering but with his father dying he'd had to go out to work.

'We've no money.'

'You'd get a loan,' said Jess.

'My dad would never go for it,' said Laurie. 'He wants me to get out and start working when I'm sixteen.' He'd said a smart girl like her should have no problem!

'It's your life,' said Jess.

Laurie thought it was easy for her to say that! They didn't have the same money problems in their house. Jess was right, though: it *was* her life. Fired up by the thought, she decided to tackle her father the first chance she had.

It came quicker than she'd expected. He was sitting by the fire reading his racing-form paper when she came in. He'd been coming home from the pub earlier these last few nights. Lack of money, she presumed.

She made them some tea and sat down opposite him.

'Dad,' she said, plunging straight in, 'I'd like to stay on at school and go to college afterwards to study music.'

He lowered his paper. 'What in the name for? You can earn money singing as it is.'

'There's more to it than singing at gigs. If I had some training I might be able to go further.'

'Like where? Opera?'

'Who knows?'

'Catch yourself on, girl! You can forget any stupid notions about college!'

'They're not stupid.'

'I've not got a job. Or have you forgotten?'

'How could I?'

'And your brother can't get work either.'

Laurie felt her blood beginning to boil. It was always the same when you suggested anything in this house. Put it down! 'So I'm supposed to work to keep you in pints, is that it? So that you can drink till you're paralytic and boak all over yourself!'

She jumped up and so did he. They faced one another.

'Don't you dare speak to me like that!' He lifted his hand and struck her hard across the face. She felt as if the ceiling had come down on her.

She drew back, trembling. She knew she'd gone

too far but she hadn't thought he would strike her. He'd hit Dave often before but never her. She put a hand to her cheek. It felt on fire.

She ran from the room.

'Stuck-up wee cow,' she heard her father mutter before she slammed the door behind her.

She went upstairs and into her room and flung herself face downward on the bed. The tears came then. A minute or two later there was a knock on the door.

'Laurie?' said her father, opening the door a crack. 'I didn't mean to hit you. It was just you speaking to me like that. It gave me a queer shock like. You've never spoken to me that way before. You're still your daddy's wee girl, aren't you? I'm sorry, I tell you, love. Laurie, do you forgive me?'

She couldn't speak. She just couldn't speak. He went out and closed the door.

NINE

Laurie's top lip was swollen and her eyes were red and puffy. She hadn't gone to school that day. How could she, looking the way she did? She'd stayed in her room, avoiding her father, and come out only in the afternoon to meet Jess coming from school.

They'd taken the train out to Holywood together and come for a walk along the shore path. Laurie was glad of the fresh sea air.

'Don't give up the idea of college,' Jess was urging her. 'I wouldn't if I were you.'

'No, I guess you wouldn't.' Laurie felt tired, even though she'd done nothing all day. She sighed, then said slowly, 'Maybe you're right, I shouldn't either. I'd have to leave home but.'

'Well, do it! You could live on a loan and earn other bits and pieces. You could get gigs at clubs in the country districts.'

'With you accompanying me on the guitar!'

'And Neal on the fiddle!'

By the time they'd walked back to the station Laurie was feeling more cheerful.

'Thanks for letting me talk to you, Jess.'

'What else are friends for?' Jess gave her a hug. They were becoming really close, she and her Protestant cousin.

'You take care!' said Laurie. 'You'd better not get caught with Barney!'

Jess grinned.

'You like the danger part, don't you?' said Laurie. 'Meeting in secret? Wouldn't suit me. I've enough bothers in my life as it is.'

Jess admitted that it did add a little excitement.

Laurie left on the Belfast train and Jess went to wait for Barney.

The lights of his bicycle heralded his arrival. It had grown dark in the last half-hour. He rang his bell and waved. She went forward to meet him. They were also becoming close, the two of them.

He threw down his bike to kiss her. His breath smelt of spearmint and his cheeks were fresh from the air.

The hour they had together went quickly. They walked a little but didn't make a great deal of progress. They kept stopping.

They returned to the place where Barney had left his bike.

'I wish I didn't have to go home,' said Jess. 'But my dad will be watching out the window.'

'Where does he think you are?'

'I told him I was going to my friend Bernadette's.'

Barney asked Jess if he could see her next day and

she had to say no. The evening then went sour and they had their first row.

'I'm sorry but I can't!' she said. 'I'm going ice-skating with some friends. Anyway, I can't see you every night.'

'Why not?'

'Don't be daft!'

Up to this point their dispute had been fairly amicable.

'Couldn't I come too?' asked Barney. 'I'm a whiz on skates. Or would they mind that I'm a Prod?'

'Oh, for goodness' sake, don't start that! It's a girls' night out, stupid!'

He pouted. 'What about the next night?'

'That's our rehearsal night. We don't have long to get our tape in and we're nowhere near ready.'

'That damn song!'

'It's not a *damn* song!'

'So what about the next-again night?'

'I've got drama club.'

'Seems you don't have too much time for me then, doesn't it?' Barney picked up his bike. 'I'll see you one of these days, I guess. When you can fit me in.'

He leapt on to the saddle and went pedalling off, leaving her standing in the middle of the path like a lemon! The nerve of him!

So he was in the huff! She had other things to do with her time and if he didn't understand that then to pot with him!

She went up the hill, to find her father standing at their gate.

'I was just round at Bernadette's,' he said.

'Oh,' she said.

'I had to take the church newspaper to her parents.'

Jess had said she would deliver it but she'd forgotten.

'You haven't been with Bernadette all evening, have you?'

'Well, no.'

'So who have you been with? You were out with a boy, weren't you?'

'So what's wrong with that? I'm old enough.'

'Maybe you are. But I want to know why you told me a lie.'

'I didn't want to worry you.'

'Was it someone I wouldn't approve of then? So who was he?'

'No one you know.'

'Someone from school? Holywood?'

'No.'

'What do you call him?'

'Bernard.' That was true. It was the name Barney had been christened by.

'Bernard what?'

Jess couldn't remember. 'Doyle,' she said, giving him a predominantly Catholic surname. That should mollify her father to some extent. He wouldn't be *exactly* against her having a Protestant boyfriend, but he'd prefer that she didn't. Sticking to her own kind would be safer. Didn't he know that from his own experience?

'You'll need to bring him home sometime so that we can meet him. You know we prefer you to bring your friends home than hang about the streets.'

'It's not serious. I may not even be seeing him again anyway.'

'You're never in these days. I hope you're not letting your schoolwork slip?'

She went in to start on it now, but since the evening was half over she didn't manage to finish it and had to do it on the bus in the morning.

'Have you done your homework?' she asked Danny.

'Sort of,' he said, and looked out of the window.

Danny stayed by the school gate while Jess went on into the playground to join Bernadette. The minute the girls met up they started yacking. About boys, no doubt! Jess yacked half the evening on the phone. Danny waited until the bell rang, then he joined the back of the lines straggling towards the building.

His first lesson of the morning was double maths and that went not too badly for him, then he had French.

He quite liked the language. They'd been to France last year on holiday. But he wasn't happy when he was asked to stand up and read a passage aloud. He felt his face heat up and his hands begin to tremble as they held the book. Sitting in the desk in front of him was Gerald Riley, one of his tormentors, who, since Mr Duggan had intervened, had been giving him a wide berth. Nevertheless, none of them missed a chance to get a dig in at him.

While he was reading, Riley kept twisted round in his seat making piggy eyes. Danny tried to ignore him, to keep his eyes on the book. His voice faltered, he stumbled over a word that he knew and could pronounce perfectly well, and lost the place. Several of his classmates tittered.

'That's fine, Danny, thank you,' said Miss O'Donnell, the teacher.

He sat down. He knew it hadn't been fine. Someone else was asked to read. Danny lost track of what was going on.

At the end of the lesson, when he was passing the teacher's desk, she motioned him over.

'Are you able to follow what we're doing, Danny?'

'Yes.'

'That's good,' said Miss O'Donnell, as if she were not convinced. 'If you have any problems you must come to me.' She nodded, dismissing him.

He walked out into the corridor. She probably thought he was stupid! Everybody thought he was stupid.

At break he drifted down through the playground towards the gate. He gazed out into the street. There lay freedom. He sighed. So close and yet so far.

He glanced back. Nobody was paying him any attention. Nobody was interested in him. He looked up the road and down the road. There was not a soul about.

Swiftly he made up his mind. He slid out through the gate and, taking to his heels, fled.

He didn't stop running until he was at least half a mile from the school, then he stopped. He was panting too much. He had to take out his inhaler. A few inhalations, and his breathing eased.

Now he listened. No sounds of school, no ringing

of bells or shrieking of kids reached him. He had escaped!

He wandered about before coming on a children's playground. It was empty. The swings hung limply from their chains. A bird perched on the motionless roundabout, his head cocked, listening. Danny went in and sat on one of the swings, letting his body move idly to and fro and his feet scuff the ground. The bird flew up and off into the greyness of the sky.

Danny leaned back and pulled on the chains, and gradually, as he went up, his feet cleared the ground. He continued to go up and up, higher and higher, into the still, damp air; and the stand creaked, and the ground tilted beneath him. He was leaning so far back now that his legs were almost in a straight line with his body.

'Hey, you up there!'

The chains juddered as he looked down. Below stood a woman in a red hat holding a small child by the hand.

'Want to kill yourself, son?'

He came down quite fast and soon his feet were grazing the earth again.

'What are you doing in here?' demanded the woman. 'You're far too big for these swings.'

He leapt off his perch, leaving the swing swaying behind him.

From the park he headed for the Newtownards Road. His cousin Dave lived down that way. He wouldn't mind seeing him again. They'd got on OK. Dave would be free too. They could do something together, go somewhere.

He walked the length of the road and went on into the centre of town but saw no sign of his cousin.

At the end of the afternoon, when Jess was standing at the gate with Bernadette, she happened to glance up the road and see Danny coming running at full tilt. He didn't notice her, he had his eye fixed on his bus. He leapt on to it just as it was revving up to take off.

'I think Danny may have mitched school,' Jess said to Bernadette.

He denied it when she challenged him later, but she knew from the evasive look in his eye that he wasn't telling the truth.

'Don't dare do it again!'

'All right! All right!' He held up his hands in surrender.

'Promise you won't!'

'I promise.'

'Where did you go?'

'Nowhere.'

'There's no such place as nowhere.'

The phone rang and Danny dived into the hall to grab it.

'It's for you,' he said, returning. 'Sounds like your lover boy.'

'What are you talking about?'

'I've seen you on the shore path. Smooch, smooch.'

Jess went to the phone.

'Hi,' said Barney.

'Hi,' she said offhandedly.

'Sorry I zoomed off like that last night.'

They made up.

Danny was still hanging about when Jess came off the phone.

'I won't tell,' he said meaningfully.

She got the message! She had something on him but he had something on her. Blackmail! It seemed to be rife in the family at present, what with her father being blackmailed by Sammy, and now her brother putting the screws on her!

TEN

When Sammy came to the door Laurie was at home trying to catch up on her work. Her parents were both out and Dave was up in his room playing tapes. She had been enjoying peace and quiet in the living room for once. And then the knock came.

She opened the door to see Sammy standing on the pavement, his booted feet planted astride, giving out the message that he'd not be budged until he'd got what he'd come for. Laurie's first instinct was to close the door fast but if she'd tried to he'd have put out a boot to jam it.

What *had* he come for?

'How're you doin', Laurie?' he said.

'Fine,' she said, her fingers gripping the edge of the door.

'I hear you're coming on at the singing. I could maybe get you a few wee jobs.'

'I don't have much time,' she said awkwardly. Surely he hadn't called to say that!

'Is your brother in?'

'Dave?'

'You've only got the one, haven't you?' Sammy smiled. 'Is he in?' Seeing her hesitate, he said, 'I've a feeling he must be. Haven't seen him out on the streets the day. I wondered if he would be lying low. Give him a call, would you? Tell him I'm wanting a word.'

She pushed the door to, letting it click shut. She ran up the stairs.

'Dave,' she said, 'Sammy wants a word with you.'

Dave looked petrified. 'Tell him I'm out.'

'I can't. He knows you're in. You'd better go and speak to him or he'll kick the door in.'

Dave got up and went down. He had the face on him of someone going to his doom.

'Come on out on the pavement a minute, Dave,' said Sammy. 'You go on in, Laurie. This doesn't concern you. Your brother and I have a wee bit of business to discuss.'

Laurie closed the door and went racing back up the stairs to her parents' bedroom, which overlooked the front street. She opened the window as quietly as she could. Dave and Sammy were standing on the pavement below.

'Have you thought then, Dave?' asked Sammy.

'Thought?' stammered Dave.

'Now don't be trying to tell me you forgot the wee chat we had the other night? About the job?'

Dave gulped and said, 'I'm not wanting to do it, Sammy.'

'You're not?' Sammy feigned surprise. 'But you remember those tablets I gave you the other day?

There were six of them, if my memory serves me right.'

'I put them in the bin,' said Dave quickly.

'Do you tell me? I heard something different. I heard you sold them.' Sammy's voice changed. 'You did, didn't you, Magowan?'

'Well, it was just this fella came along –'

'Fellas always come along! So I think you owe me now.'

'But I haven't got the money, honest I haven't.'

'That's too bad, isn't it? You know there's no such thing as a free lunch? So maybe you should just reconsider that wee job.'

'I told you I'm not wanting it. I'm not wanting to push –'

'Now, now, lad, no need to get het up. Think about it again. I'll give you one more chance. Once you've thought, I've a feeling you'll see things my way. You know where to find me.' Sammy tapped Dave lightly on the shoulder. 'And I know where to find you.'

Sammy moved on up the street. Dave went back into the house. His sister was coming down the stairs.

'I heard every word,' she said, 'so you needn't bother telling me any lies.'

'What am I going to do?' Dave went into the living room and collapsed into a chair, huddling down into it as if he'd like to make himself smaller. Or invisible.

'You see how one stupid thing leads to another.'

'Cut the preaching!'

'OK! But you asked me what you should do!'

Laurie paced up and down trying to think. The

room was not very big and there was too much furniture in it for its size, so you soon ended up banging your shins. 'What about going up to Ballymena to stay with Uncle Billy and Aunt Rita for a while? It'd get you out of the way. You could lie low. And you like the country.'

'I can't stick her but.'

'Beggars can't be choosers.'

Laurie lifted her jacket from a chair.

'You going out?' asked Dave.

'Yes. Why don't you? Do you good instead of sitting there getting square eyes in front of the telly.'

'I went up for Barney earlier. He was all ponced up ready to go out "on a date". With our fancy cousin.'

'Why do you have to be nasty *all* the time?'

Laurie left.

She took a bus downtown. Neal was waiting for her in the café. He'd phoned earlier to say he'd had an idea for the next part of their song and would like to go over it with her. He'd been working on the chorus.

'How about this? "Two worlds in disarray, the secret broke away. Two worlds that belonged –"' He broke off. 'I haven't got any further.'

She thought. '"And were silent –"'

'"For years,"' he added.

They put the four lines together.

'Two worlds in disarray
The secret broke away
Two worlds that belonged
And were silent for years.'

'That's good!' said Laurie. The song, and the competition, were beginning to excite her.

They sat for a couple of hours, talking about work and school and families. Laurie told Neal about Dave's new dilemma.

Neal suggested getting the money together to pay Sammy for the drugs. 'Wipe out the debt. Then he can't blackmail Dave.'

'That's if Sammy would let us pay him off.'

'It's worth trying. I could lend you the money.'

She thanked him but thought she could manage it herself. She had some money in the post office which she would prefer not to touch, given the choice.

She was saving for her future! Whatever that would be. Every time she put a couple of pounds into the bank she thought of it as helping her on the road to college. She was doing some regular baby-sitting for a couple of teachers at school. They had nice comfortable houses and she could get on with her homework and they paid her. And left her sandwiches and a flask of coffee! She felt she was being spoiled. And then they insisted on driving her home.

Neal walked her almost the whole way home, although she'd told him to leave her earlier. She didn't like him running the risk of being seen with her on her territory.

'You come into mine, don't you?' he said.

They had just passed a shop when they heard feet hitting the pavement behind them. Neal pulled her in against the wall as three boys went thundering by. In a flash they were gone, down the next side street, but not so fast that Laurie hadn't recognized them.

The shopkeeper was out on his step. 'Stop, thieves!' he yelled and waved his arms about. 'Did you see those three yobs? Stealing my cigarettes they were!'

Laurie and Dave moved along.

'That was Dave, wasn't it?' said Neal.

'Yes,' said Laurie with a sigh, 'it was Dave.'

They were almost opposite Sammy's Fish Bar. Laurie's mother caught sight of her through the window and waved. Laurie waved back but didn't cross the road. Her mother would be asking later who the boy was that she'd been with.

'Just a boy,' Laurie told her when she did ask. 'A friend.'

'What do you call him?'

'Neal.'

'Neal what?'

Laurie shrugged. 'Met him at a gig. I'm not *going* with him. We're friends, that's all, and that's the way it's going to stay.'

'You sound very sure. He was good-looking, from what I could make out. Your dad used to be quite a looker, you know. Oh, yes! The girls would give him the eye when we went dancing at the Floral Hall on a Saturday night.' Beryl's voice had softened with the reminiscence. 'He was a flashy dresser in those days.'

Even now Ed Magowan was fussy about his looks and shaved before going out to the pub. He was always on at Dave for looking scruffy.

Next day, Laurie went to the post office and drew out forty pounds. It was her mother's night off – she was going to bingo with Granny Magowan – so Laurie could go safely into the chip shop without running across her.

Betty, who stood in on her mother's off-night, was serving.

'Is Sammy in?' asked Laurie.

Betty raised an eyebrow. 'He's in his room.'

Laurie went to the door. It was made of solid wood, more solid than you'd expect to find in a fish and chip bar, and it had a spyhole set in the upper half.

She knocked and waited. She stood face on so that Sammy would be able to identify her. She imagined his pale-blue eye fringed with light-blond eyelashes squinting at her through the hole.

The door opened.

'Laurie, come on in! This is a pleasure, 'deed it is. Have you been thinking about my offer to help with your singing?'

He closed the door and waved her towards a seat. She remained standing.

'It's not about that,' she said. 'It's the money Dave owes you. For the drugs. I've got it for you.' She handed him an envelope.

'I was expecting payment in kind, not money.' Sammy looked inside. 'Forty pounds! They were worth more than that, I'm afraid.'

'That's what he got for them. So it seems fair to me.'

'You're quite a girl, Laurie Magowan! I wish I had a sister like you.' He tapped the envelope against his chin and frowned. 'OK, then, I'll take it, for your sake.'

'Thanks,' she muttered, a word she'd never thought

she'd have to say to Sammy. And she didn't want him to do anything for her sake in case he thought that put her in his debt. 'You'll let him off the hook, then?' She backed towards the door, getting ready to exit.

'This time. But he'd better watch it in future.'

'I'll tell him,' she said.

ELEVEN

Danny didn't keep his word.

On her way out of school Jess bumped into his form teacher.

'Danny not well again today, Jess?' asked Mrs Ryan.

Jess gave a start, then recovered herself quickly to say, 'No, he wasn't feeling too great this morning.'

'He's falling behind with his work. Maybe I should send some home with you? Come and see me tomorrow.'

Jess stood at the gate, scanning the pavement in both directions. What a brat! She didn't know why she was bothering to cover for him. It wasn't because she was worried that he would tell on her about Barney. If he did she would have just to ride it out, though she wouldn't relish all the ructions it would cause in the family.

She waited until all the buses had gone and the playground was empty, then she went up to the café on the main road where she'd arranged to meet Laurie and Barney. She told them why she was late.

'Where could Danny have gone?' asked Laurie.

Jess didn't have any idea, that was the trouble. But one thing she did know was that he would end up in deep trouble if he went on this way.

'He might have gone to the rail station, thinking he'd missed the school bus,' suggested Barney.

It was the only thing they could think of, so they took a bus downtown.

There was no sign of Danny inside the station. The trains to Holywood went every half-hour. They waited until the next one filled up and took off.

Barney and Laurie went back outside to keep watch and Jess rang home in case Danny might already be there. She heard her voice in a plummy accent chanting, 'This is the answering machine for Tommy, Maeve, Jess and Danny Magowan. We can't come to the phone right now but if you'd like to leave a message please do so after the tone.' She sounded a right eejit! She must change it. She left a message to say that she was in Belfast and would be home soon.

She went back to join Barney and Laurie and found them talking to Danny and Dave!

'Look who's here!' said Barney, trying to lighten the moment.

Jess was too wound up for light to penetrate. 'Danny, where on earth have you been?'

'You don't have to shout!'

'Don't I? I've been running about half-demented looking for you. You mitched again, didn't you?'

'OK, so I did. So what?'

'So *what*? Where have you been?'

'With Dave.'

'Dave!' Jess glared now at him. He was standing there looking amused. '*All* day?'

'I bumped into him on the Newtonards Road,' said Danny.

'What were you doing there?'

Danny shrugged. 'I was just there. Look, I didn't mean to come back late but Dave's watch is broken and I didn't have mine on.'

'His head'll get broken if he takes you off again.'

The smile slipped from Dave's face and he straightened up from his slouch. He came towards Jess. Barney stepped smartly between them, separating them.

'Cool it, both of you!'

'Cool it?' said Dave, wrestling free from Barney's grasp. 'I'll buckle her gob for her if she's not careful.' He raised his fist.

'Dave!' cried Laurie.

'Just you try it, Dave Magowan!' cried Jess. Barney kept a firm hold of her.

'Dave didn't take me off, Jess,' said Danny. 'I *went* with him. I wanted to go.'

'He'd have known you were mitching school. He shouldn't have encouraged you!'

'I didn't encourage him!' said Dave. 'He was on his own. He was fed up. He might have got into worse trouble if he hadn't come with me.'

'So you were playing the social worker, were you? Seeing he didn't get into trouble. Well, he's in plenty now!'

'Let's go home, Dave.' Laurie put her hand on her brother's arm. She looked troubled.

'Yes, go on home, Dave,' said Barney.

'You'll not tell me what to do, Barney Dunlop!'

'*Dave!*' said Laurie.

He hesitated, then he turned and went with her.

'Thanks, Dave,' Danny called after him. 'That was a great day we had. See you again!'

'Not if I can help it!' said Jess.

'You can't choose my friends,' said Danny.

'Friends! Where did you go with him? And don't bother telling any more lies!'

'Down the old docks. We weren't doing anything wrong.'

'Except that you should have been at school. How did you get past security?'

'Easy enough. We just waited till the guard was looking the other way.'

Jess didn't doubt that Dave would be skilful at getting into places where he shouldn't be.

'You going to tell on me, Jess?'

'I don't know. Have those boys been bullying you again?'

'They don't *do* anything. It's the way they look at me and snigger. Snigger, snigger, snigger! Like three snorty pigs! I wish somebody would roast them over a hot fire till they squeal!'

'How about if I teach you judo, Danny?' offered Barney. 'Then you could deal with them if you had to.'

'Shouldn't think I'd be any good at it.'

'Stop running yourself down!' said Jess crossly. She

was becoming exasperated with him. 'Make up your mind you will be good at it! Come on, let's go for the train.'

They had just missed one and had to wait twenty-five minutes for the next. They reached home at half-past seven to find their mother leaping about the way a hen was supposed to on a hot griddle. Their father had gone out looking for them.

'You'd think we were five years old,' said Jess. Both their parents panicked far too early in any situation. She was sure they'd imagined them squashed to death on the roads, kidnapped, caught in a hail of terrorist bullets a dozen times over. 'We've just been down-town. Didn't you get my message?'

'That was almost two hours ago. And you said nothing about Danny.' His mother surveyed him. 'Where's your bag?' It was typical of her to go off at a tangent.

Jess registered for the first time that he didn't have his bag with him. So did he.

The door opened to admit their father, who proceeded to give Danny the third degree. Where had he gone after school? Why hadn't he come home on the school bus? Was he with Jess the whole time? Danny began to flounder.

'I've a feeling I'm not hearing the whole truth about all this,' said their father.

'All right,' Danny said to Jess, 'go ahead and tell them! I don't care!' He left the room and went dashing up the stairs. They heard his door slam.

And so Jess told them. It was too big a problem for her to keep to herself any longer.

Her mother couldn't believe Danny would do such a thing. He'd always been such an honest boy! Her father said he would go up and talk to him.

'Don't shout at him now, Tommy,' cautioned his wife. 'It won't do any good.'

'I never shout!' He reduced the volume of his voice. He shook his head. 'I just can't understand it – a son of mine doing this.'

That was getting to him! That *his* son was playing hookey. Jess bit her tongue to stop herself saying so. There was no point in winding him up any further.

'He was being bullied at school,' she said.

'He'll have to learn to stand up for himself then, won't he? I had to when I was at school.'

But he wasn't able to stand up to Sammy, was he? That was something else she couldn't say.

'He's been ill, Tommy,' Maeve reminded him.

'I don't want to be hard on him, but he's got to get back to leading a normal life. He can't play the invalid for ever.'

'He wasn't playing, Tommy. How can you say that?'

'Don't you two start arguing now!' said Jess.

'You stay out of this!' said her father. 'You've caused enough trouble not telling us before.'

'Let's think of Danny now, Tommy,' said Maeve appeasingly.

He sighed. 'I'll do what I can.'

Danny was lying stretched out on his bed. His father sat himself down on the chair beside it.

'You realize cutting school's a serious business, don't you, Danny?'

'I guess.'

'You guess! Now I know you've not been well, but you do have to go to school and get an education.' Danny made no response. Tommy laboured on. 'The law requires you to get an education. And if you don't, it's me that'll get summoned. You do understand that, don't you?' he demanded, raising his voice, then, remembering, he dropped it again. 'Have you anything to say to me?' It seemed not. Tommy went on again. 'It's not nice being bullied, I'm not saying it is, but they've not actually touched you, have they?' He got up abruptly. 'If you won't take any notice of what I have to say, I'll just have to let the headmaster deal with you.'

Tommy met his daughter on the top landing.

'I can't do a thing with that brother of yours,' he declared. 'It's like talking to a stone wall!'

Jess looked in on Danny.

'What *are* you going to do?' she asked.

'I'm not going to mitch again! But I wasn't going to tell him that.'

'Where did you leave your bag, by the way?'

'I'm not sure.'

Jess groaned. 'Better try to think!'

Danny's chest was beginning to wheeze. She left him and went to ring Laurie.

'Could you ask Dave if he knows where Danny left his bag?'

'All right. Look, Jess, it wasn't Dave's fault that Danny mitched school.' Laurie's voice had a cool edge to it, Jess thought.

'I know that. But he shouldn't have let Danny go with him to the docks.'

'I'll tell him about the bag,' said Laurie, and rang off.

TWELVE

'Who was that on the phone?' asked Dave.

'Jess,' said Laurie. 'She wanted to know if you had any idea where Danny might have left his bag.'

'Haven't the faintest. You know, she had a bleeding nerve trying to blame me! You'd think I'd been standing at his school gate trying to tempt him away. What does she think I am!'

'It was a damn stupid idea, mind you, letting him go off with you.' Although Laurie had defended him to Jess, she did think he'd behaved stupidly. But she also thought Jess was trying to put too much blame on him. Jess had annoyed her when she'd said his head would get broken if he took Danny away again! After all, it *was* Danny who had mitched.

'The kid hates school,' said Dave. 'I was doing him a favour taking him with me. Other days he says he's just been wandering around the streets.'

'Jess does go over the top at times.'

'Bitch! I don't know what Barney sees in her. And her a Mick!'

'You're just bothered because she's come between you.'

'I hardly see him these days. It's different from when he was going with other girls. Next thing you know he'll be living with her and swinging incense.'

'I doubt that.'

'Well, stuff him!' Dave got up and fiddled with the window cord. His body looked taut with frustration.

'You should find yourself a girl of your own.'

'I've no money for girls.' He pursed his lips. 'They seem to think they're something special.'

'Who? Girls?'

'No! Uncle Tommy's lot. Even the kid. Maybe they need – well, sort of puncturing a bit.'

'What do you mean by that?' Laurie felt alarmed.

'Nothing.'

'You'd better not!'

'What could I do to them? Couldn't lend us a couple of quid, could you? No, don't suppose you could.'

'I certainly could not! I've just paid Sammy forty pounds to get you off the hook, let me remind you!'

'I know!' He held up his hands. 'That was good of you, Laurie. One day –'

'Oh, yes! When your ship comes sailing up the Lough carrying gold bars! You'll end up sounding like Dad if you're not careful.'

'I'm going out.' He made for the door.

'Stay away from Gregg and Jamieson!'

He didn't answer.

Laurie took her guitar from its case and played the tune for their song. 'You are my friend for evermore . . .' Was it possible that she and Jess could be friends for evermore? They might be related by blood, but there were so many differences between them. To begin with, Jess lived in a posh, detached house with a big garden, while she lived in this dump with a smelly backyard! 'Stop it, Laurie Magowan!' she had to tell herself.

She was restless now and didn't feel like spending the evening between these four walls. She wondered if she could phone Neal and ask if he'd like to meet for coffee. He'd phoned her, after all, so why shouldn't she phone him?

His mother answered. 'Who shall I say it is?'

'Laura.'

'We met the other night, Laura, didn't we? How are you?'

'Fine, thank you.'

Neal's voice came in behind his mother's.

'Yes, it's for you, Neal. Hope to see you again sometime, Laura.'

'Goodbye, Mrs O'Shea.'

'Hello, Laura,' said Neal.

'I'm down in the dumps. Do you fancy meeting for coffee?'

'Sure thing. Meet you at the usual place?'

So they had a usual place! That made Laurie a little nervous. She gave her hair a good brush and put on some eyeshadow.

Granny Magowan was standing at her door watching the night when Laurie went along the street.

'Is that you, Laurie? Where are you off to?'

'Just downtown.'

'Meeting a fella, eh?'

'A friend.'

'That's what they all say. Mind you, you might as well have a good time while you're young. Once you get married and settled down it's a different story.'

'I'm not thinking of getting married, Granny!'

'Glad to hear it. I saw that brother of yours a few minutes ago. Went off with them two bad eggs, Gregg and Jamieson.'

Oh well, thought Laurie, what could she do about it? She wasn't his keeper.

'I must go, Granny.'

'Aye, don't keep him waiting too long. A few minutes though, so as he'll not feel too sure of you.'

Passing the chip-shop window Laurie saw her mother, bright red and shiny in the face, feverishly shovelling chips into bags and spraying them with salt and vinegar. She was determined not to end up like that! She said so to Neal.

'That's why you've got to stick to your idea of college,' he said.

They had a good evening together, easy and relaxed. Nobody bothered them. Nobody knew them there. The café was busy, with young people mostly, talking and laughing and enjoying themselves.

Neal walked her back afterwards. It was a fine night, with a sprinkling of stars to be seen and the beginnings of a moon. They stopped on Queen's Bridge and looked at the lights glinting on the Lough.

'It looks great, doesn't it?' said Neal.

They leaned their arms side by side on the parapet. Laurie felt a light breeze lifting her hair. Neal glanced sideways at her and for a moment she didn't move. Then she stepped back, hugging her arms across her chest. The moment had felt dangerous.

'It's getting chilly,' she said.

They moved on. They didn't say much now. Neal kept his thoughts to himself and she kept hers to herself. Hers were confused.

'I'll be all right now,' she said, as they drew close to her street.

'I'll see you to the corner.'

A pub door swung open, letting out the smell of smoke and beer and the clamour of voices. It also let out Ed Magowan and his drinking pal, Frankie. Ed stopped dead when he sighted his daughter.

'Is that you, Laurie? What are you doing here?'

'Walking home. What does it look like I'm doing?' She spoke mildly, however. Neither of them had referred to their row of the other evening, though her father had been avoiding looking at her straight on. He had his eye now on Neal. 'Dad,' she said, 'this is my friend Neal.'

'How do you do, Mr Magowan?' said Neal.

Ed Magowan grunted, his mouth full of a dozen unspoken questions. To Laurie he said, 'You'd better get on home or you'll never be up for school in the morning. Tell your mother I'll not be long.'

He rejoined Frankie and they crossed the road to enter another pub. They wove a little as they walked.

'It's as well seeing he doesn't have to get up in the morning!' said Laurie.

The scream of a siren turned their heads. A police car with its blue light flashing swept past at high speed, followed by a wailing fire engine. Sirens in the city were not unusual, though they always made Laurie shiver a little with apprehension.

They said good night and Neal waited on the corner until he saw her go into her house.

Beryl Magowan was home, drinking tea, with her feet up.

'You're out late, Laurie. I thought you'd homework?'

'Are you really bothered about my homework?'

'Of course. We want you to do well at school.'

'So that I can leave as soon as possible?'

'Let's not start all that up again!'

'No, let's not!'

'I'd love for you to be able to stay on, Laurie, but we need the money.'

They heard the outside door open.

'I hope that's Dave,' said Beryl. 'It's time he was in and all. I don't like him out late on the streets.'

Dave came in, a pink flush warming his cheeks.

'You look as if you've been running,' said his mother.

'The rain's coming on.' He went to the sink and filled the kettle, keeping his back to them. He didn't look wet.

'I'll not bother asking where you were,' said his mother. 'For I know what answer I'll get – out! It's a great place, out!'

'I'm away to bed.' Laurie gave her brother a thoughtful look. He'd been up to something! 'Good night, Mum. Good night, Dave.'

He didn't answer.

THIRTEEN

Jess had also spent the evening in Belfast, with Barney.

They went for a pizza and then wandered round the town looking in shop windows picking out holidays they'd like to go on. Two weeks in Thailand, ten days in Bali, a weekend in Paris.

'I'd settle for that,' said Barney. 'Guess you've been? To Paris?'

'Uhuh.' She played it down.

They then chose the clothes they would buy for their trips. Jess liked the way Barney entered into the fantasy with her.

'I suppose you can get what clothes you want?' he said. 'With your mum having her own shop.'

'I can't get *everything* I want!' said Jess. 'We're not *rich*, you know.' Though he probably thought they were.

His mother cleaned offices. She left home at half-past five in the morning, which meant that no one but him was in the house when he got up for school. There had never been any mention of a father.

It was such a nice night that they walked on and on, crossing the river into East Belfast, Barney's territory. He kept his arm around Jess's waist.

They came to the murals at 'Freedom Corner'. Jess studied the clenched fist and the soldier with his rifle and the Red Hand of Ulster.

'"We will maintain our freedom,"' she read. To Barney she said, 'No one's trying to take it away.'

'Says who! We would lose it if we were forced to go in with the Republic.'

She laughed. 'I don't think we'll bother getting into all that!'

'We're not wanting to quarrel, are we?'

'Certainly not!'

It was too good a night for arguments, especially political ones. They continued along the road and, taking a detour, found themselves close to Tommy Magowan's garage.

'Do you want to see it?' said Jess.

'Yeah, why not?'

The place was locked up, of course, so all they could do was look from the outside. The perimeter fence was high, as was the side gate.

'Looks a pretty good business,' said Barney.

'My dad's always muttering on about going bankrupt.' Jess never knew whether to take him seriously or not.

'I guess people have to borrow a lot to go into business.' Barney then said abruptly, 'My dad's in jail. He'll be getting out next year.'

Jess got a shock when he said that. She didn't know anyone in prison or anyone who had relatives in prison.

'Does that bother you?' He let his arm drop from her waist, as if telling her she was free to go if she wanted to.

'Why should it?' she said. But it did bother her, in spite of the fact that she was trying to tell herself that it shouldn't. What would her dad say if he knew she was going out with the son of a jailbird! But *Barney* wasn't a jailbird. 'I mean, *you* haven't done anything. So what difference should it make to us?'

'I don't know. I thought it might.'

'What did he do?'

'He took a car.'

That didn't seem to her to be the worst offence in the world, not after the crimes they'd seen here in Northern Ireland. Not that she could approve of it.

'It can't have been easy on you, Barney,' she said softly. She felt soft towards him. What an awful thing to have to cope with!

'No, it wasn't easy. It still isn't. It doesn't go away.'

'It *doesn't* make any difference to us,' she said.

He bent his head and kissed her.

'You're a great girl, Jess. You know I'm crazy about you, don't you?'

She had a pretty good idea. He waited for her up the road from school every day, phoned at least twice every evening and came out to meet her at the ring of the telephone.

They had moved further along the pavement and

were standing under an overhanging tree when they heard footsteps. Three boys had turned into the street.

'Dave!' said Barney quietly.

The boys were on the opposite side of the road. They were sauntering along, taking their time, eyeing the garage closely.

'What are they up to?' whispered Jess.

Barney shook his head.

A car was coming. The noise of the engine had alerted the boys and they veered sharply to cross the street. It was a police car. The three were now walking briskly away from the scene, as if they had somewhere definite to go and were not just loitering. The police car drove on.

'That may have saved us a bit of trouble, do you think?' said Jess.

'I hope so,' said Barney.

It was late, time for her to head back to Holywood. Barney saw her on to the train.

She exchanged a few words with her father when she got in about lateness and lack of sleep and lack of application to schoolwork. Nothing new. She went upstairs.

She was ready for bed and coming out of the bathroom when the doorbell rang. Her father emerged from the sitting room below swearing and demanding of no one in particular who that could be bothering them at this time of night. Jess hung over the banisters to see.

'Good evening, officer,' said her father. 'Anything wrong?'

Jess ran down the stairs, saw the dark green-black

of a police uniform at the door. At the gate sat a police car with another policeman inside.

The constable on the doorstep was holding up Danny's bag. 'Is this your son's bag, Mr Magowan?'

'Looks like it. Doesn't it, Jess?'

She came forward to examine it. 'It does.'

'It's got his name in it,' said the constable. 'Danny Magowan, and his address.'

'In that case,' said Tommy, 'there's no question that it is. I didn't know Danny had lost his bag, did you, Jess?'

'Well, he did say something.' She let her voice trail off.

'Where did you find it?' asked her father.

'Down at the old docks.'

'At the docks! Danny wouldn't go to a place like that. Somebody must have nicked it and dumped it down there.'

Jess remained quiet.

'Could we have a word with him?' said the constable. 'We had to get a sniffer dog out and a bomb explosive expert standing by.'

'I suppose you would,' said Tommy. 'Jess, away up and ask Danny to come down here.'

She had to waken him. He struggled into consciousness rubbing his eyes. He jerked fully awake when she told him what was up.

'What am I going to say?'

'Just that you went down to the docks. You don't have to say who with.'

He came down in his pyjamas and told the police that he had gone to the old docks.

'What did you go there for?'

'Something to do.'

'Shouldn't you have been at school?'

'He should, officer,' put in his father. 'We're dealing with that.'

'Do you realize the fuss you've caused?' the constable asked Danny.

'Yes, sir. I'm sorry. I won't go down there again.'

'Better not!' said his father. 'We can only apologize for the trouble you've been caused, officer.'

The policemen left. Tommy Magowan rounded on Danny.

'Why *did* you go there?'

'I said.'

'I know what you said! You've never gone down the docks before, have you?'

'No.'

'You went alone, did you? You're sure?'

'Yes,' said Danny, looking away.

'It's late, Tommy,' said his mother, who had been hovering in the background. 'These kids'll never get up for school in the morning.'

Their father, for once, seemed lost for words. He went into the sitting room and poured himself a large whisky.

Danny and Jess retreated upstairs.

'You'll end up driving him to drink!' said Jess.

She was getting into bed when the doorbell rang for the second time. She pulled her dressing gown on again and went back on to the landing. Her father was coming out of the sitting room.

'What in the name is going on? A man can't get a minute's peace in his own house!' He was still cursing as he opened the door. 'Officer!' he said. 'We've just had a constable here about my son's bag.'

But the policeman had not come about a bag. Jess went half-way down the stairs.

'Are you Tommy Magowan?' asked the constable.

'Yes, that's me.'

'Are you the keyholder for the Paramount Garage?'

'I am. Why, what's happened?'

'You'd better come, Mr Magowan. Some of your cars are on fire.'

'Oh, no!' cried Jess.

'I'll be there as quick as I can!' said Tommy Magowan.

'I'll come with you, Dad,' said Jess, and went to get dressed.

They smelt the burning when they were still half a mile from the garage. By the time they reached it, the flames had been extinguished and three cars had been reduced to blackened shells. The forecourt was flooded with water from the firemen's hoses. The firemen themselves were preparing to leave.

Tommy stood on the forecourt swearing at the wrecked cars, his feet soaking up the water.

'There's nothing to be done tonight. We might as well get on home.'

Before they could make a move, a car swept in by the side gate.

'Look who's coming!' said Tommy.

Under the arc lights they saw that Sammy's frown

was black. He got out of the car and came to meet them.

'This shouldn't have happened,' he said.

'That's what I was thinking,' said Tommy.

'It was none of my men, don't be thinking that! You're under my protection, Magowan. But don't worry your head. I'll find out who done it and sort them out, never fear! If they think they can do the dirt on Sammy, they've another think coming.'

He returned to his car.

Jess thought of the three boys who'd been loitering outside earlier in the evening.

'I wouldn't like to be in the shoes of whoever did do it!' she said.

FOURTEEN

'You know the Paramount Garage, Laurie?' said her mother.

'Yes, why?'

'Three cars got burned out there last night.'

'They never did! Where did you hear that?'

'Sammy. Who else? I suspect he's got an interest in the place.'

'He's got far too many interests, that man,' said Granny Magowan, kicking off her shoes. She'd been downtown and liked to wear three-inch heels when she went out, even though they were murder on the feet. 'And none of them good.'

'I wish you didn't have to work for him, Mum,' said Laurie.

'It's a job.'

'I know! And we need the money!'

'Who doesn't?' said Granny complacently.

It was a pity her son didn't get out and earn some, thought Laurie, and spend less in the pub while he was at it.

'I wish Dave could get a job,' sighed his mother.

'He's getting to be dead lazy, so he is,' said his grandmother. 'He said he'd get my messages this morning but he never went. Typical! It'd have saved my feet. My blisters are swelling up like apricots.'

'Why does everybody pick on Dave?' demanded Laurie.

'What's up with you the day?' asked Granny. 'Ants got into your pants? So Sammy was annoyed, was he, Beryl?' she said, reverting to the previous topic. She liked to hear any gossip that was going and her daughter-in-law, by working at the chip shop, was well placed for picking it up.

'I could hear him bellowing on the phone at lunchtime.'

'He'd be calling up his troops,' said Granny, with some relish. 'Getting them out on the manhunt.'

'You know who that garage belongs to?' said Laurie. She felt like giving them a jolt. They disapproved of Sammy, feared him, like most people round about, yet they enjoyed hearing of his exploits. And her mother went on working for him. She maintained it was no business of hers what he got up to in his back shop. 'Tommy Magowan,' said Laurie. '*Our* Tommy Magowan.'

'He's not ours!' said Granny sharply. 'Anyway, how do you know that?'

'I just do.'

'You might make us a cup of tea, Laurie,' said Beryl.

'I'm going upstairs to do my homework.' Laurie lifted her bag from the floor. 'You want me to do well at school, don't you?'

'She is snarky the day,' she heard her grandmother say as she left the room. 'Must be her age.'

'She's been in a funny mood ever since she broke up with her boyfriend,' said Beryl.

After she'd done her homework, Laurie got ready to go out. They were having another rehearsal. Time was running out, the closing date for the song competition was coming up. While she changed, she hummed the chorus. '"Two worlds in disarray . . ."'

As she was brushing her hair the door opened and her mother came in. She had her chip-shop overall on and the turban over her hair that she wore to keep the smell of frying at bay.

'Where is it you go these nights, Laurie? You're not with Sharon, are you? Her mum was saying she hadn't seen you for ages.'

'If you want to know,' said Laurie, in the new, defiant mood that had taken hold of her, 'I meet Jess Magowan.'

'I knew you were up to something!' Beryl Magowan closed the door and leaned her back against it.

'I also meet her cousin Neal O'Shea.'

'Neal *O'Shea*? You don't mean those O'Sheas?'

'I do. The ones that lured Uncle Tommy away to Rome.'

'What *has* got into you?'

Laurie flicked some mascara over her eyelashes.

'Was that the boy I saw you with the other night?'

'It was.'

'You told me you weren't involved with him.'

‘I’m not. I said he was a friend. And he is, a good friend.’

‘I’ve heard that before!’

‘It’s true! I like talking to him. He listens to what you have to say. The three of us – Jess and him and I – we meet to play music together. We’re going to enter a song competition. So now you know all there is to know.’ Laurie picked up the hairbrush and resumed brushing her hair. It crackled with electricity.

‘But, Laurie, your father and your granny –’

‘OK, so they would have heart attacks if they found out. Probably best that they don’t, then.’

‘You’ve changed, so you have.’ Her mother shook her head. ‘Where is it you go to play the music?’

‘In a garage in town.’ If Laurie were to tell her exactly where, that would give *her* a heart attack. ‘Look, Mum, you can’t talk me out of going, so I wouldn’t bother trying if I were you.’

‘You’re a strong-willed girl, Laurie! But until now you’ve always been sensible. Unlike that brother of yours! I’ve never had to worry about you much before.’

‘Don’t worry now. I can take care of myself. You’d better be getting to work, hadn’t you, or Sammy will be yelling blue murder.’

The thought of Sammy and murder, blue or otherwise, made Laurie feel sick.

Neal was working late that evening. He was finishing a job for a man who needed his car first thing in the morning. His uncle had asked him to lock up.

He was alone, then, when Sammy arrived.

'Glad I caught you, O'Shea. I was wanting a word.'

Neal wiped his hands on a rag and straightened up from the car.

'You have a key to the side gate, don't you?' asked Sammy.

Neal nodded.

'Where were you last night?'

'In town.'

'Do you say? You weren't round here by any chance?'

Neal frowned. 'You're not trying to say –'

'That you started the fires? It's a possibility.'

'Why would I do that? It's my uncle's garage!'

'Insurance?' suggested Sammy.

'That'll only pay for the three cars to be replaced.'

'Maybe youse were thinking the whole garage would go up but the fire engines arrived too quick.'

'This is crazy!'

'Is it? Your uncle's been having cash-flow problems, hasn't he? I saw you last night, O'Shea, in our district. I saw you passing my shop. You were walking pretty fast.'

'I was wanting to get home.'

'Funny way to get home to the Short Strand from downtown. You were coming from the wrong direction. I'll be going now, O'Shea. I've got other inquiries to make, but I'll be keeping my eye on you. Remember that!'

Neal met the girls on Albert Bridge.

'I've been working late,' he said. 'Haven't had time

to go home. I'll leave you at the garage and then I'll go for my fiddle.'

They were all quiet tonight on the way there and didn't talk much.

'Lock the door behind me,' said Neal when he'd opened up. 'And don't open it to anyone but me.'

As if they would!

They locked the door. Jess made no move to take her guitar from its case.

'Have you heard about the fires at our garage?' she asked.

'Yes,' said Laurie guardedly.

'I think your Dave might have been involved.'

'Why do you say that?'

'Barney and I saw him earlier on. Hanging round the garage with those two friends of his.'

'That doesn't prove anything!'

'Maybe not. But they could have been casing the place and then come back later.'

'You don't know that. You're just guessing!'

'Seems a reasonable guess to me, from what I've heard about him.'

'Heard from whom? Barney wouldn't slag Dave off. Why are you so keen to? You blamed him for taking Danny away. He was only trying to help. He was worried Danny might get into trouble.'

'So he's a wee angel, is he? Rescuing the lost and lonely? Pardon me if I can't see his halo! He's a yob!'

They glared at each other.

'How *dare* you say that?' Laurie was spluttering. 'You're just a stuck-up bitch! You think you're wonderful, don't you, because you live in a big house and your father owns a garage!'

'And you're so self-righteous you're not true! Little Laurie Two Shoes!'

'I don't know why I thought we could ever be friends!'

'It was stupid, wasn't it!'

Neal knocked on the door, silencing them. 'It's me,' he said.

Jess opened the door.

'What's been going on?' he asked, trying to sound jovial.

'I don't feel like playing tonight.' Jess lifted her guitar case. 'I'm tired, after being up half the night. I'll see you, Neal.' She left without looking at Laurie.

'I don't feel like singing either,' said Laurie. 'Anyway, there's no point in going on now. I shouldn't think we'll be going in for any song competition. "You are my friend for evermore!" That's a laugh.'

'Were you quarrelling, the two of you?'

'We've fallen out,' said Laurie, and burst into tears.

Neal put his arms round her. 'You'll make up, you'll see.'

'I told her she was a stuck-up bitch.'

'She can be at times!'

'She said I was self-righteous.'

'I wouldn't agree. Stubborn, maybe.' He smiled. 'You can both be stubborn.'

He had brought a flask of coffee back from the house with him. They sat on a couple of tyres to drink it.

'You're quiet tonight,' said Laurie. 'What's up?'

'It's nothing.' He shrugged.
'Come on, tell me! I tell you things.'
'I had a visit from Sammy,' he said.

FIFTEEN

After her row with Laurie, Jess went home and went to bed. She was seething. The nerve of Laurie, calling her a stuck-up bitch! So she'd been resenting the fact that her family was better off than hers! Yet Jess felt she'd always tried not to make anything of it. And it wasn't her fault, was it, that her father had done well for himself and Laurie's hadn't?

'If anybody phones, tell them I'm asleep,' she told her mother before going upstairs. 'Don't call me no matter who it is.' If Laurie phoned to apologize, she could sweat a while.

Danny came into her room to ask for help with his French homework.

'I couldn't help anyone with anything tonight. I'm knackered. Sit down a minute, though, Danny.'

He perched on the end of her bed.

'What did you talk about to Dave? Yesterday.'

Danny became cagey. 'Nothing much. Cars and that.'

'Did he tell you he used to go joyriding?'

Jess was sorry that she'd brought it up, for Danny was looking interested. She didn't want to make Dave into some kind of daredevil hero. Joyriding was the kind of thing Danny would never dare to do himself but would admire someone else doing from a distance.

'Did Laurie tell you that?'

'No. Barney.'

'Your boyfriend?' Danny grinned. 'Did he do it too?'

'Couple of times. But he wouldn't do it now. He's far too smart.' Jess feared she might be sounding preachy, but she carried on. 'He said he was going through a stupid stage at the time.' It had been when his father had just gone to jail and Barney was unsettled. This piece of information she kept to myself.

'Dave didn't say anything about joyriding to me.' Danny got up.

'Don't have anything more to do with him, Danny, *please*! You could end up in really bad trouble.'

Danny went off to his room and Jess put out the light and dropped into sleep like a stone falling to the bottom of a deep pit.

She went straight home after school next day and did her history homework, leaving the maths until later.

'You're not going out again?' said her mother, seeing her take her jacket from the hallstand after supper. 'You're never in these days.'

'I'm only going out for an hour, Mum. Promise!'

'It had better just be for an hour,' said her father, appearing in the sitting-room doorway. 'If you don't do well enough in your exams, you can leave school when you're sixteen. I'm not going to support you so that you can fool around.'

'All right!' said Jess, and made her escape.

Barney was sitting on a rock down at the shore, waiting for her.

Arms entwined, they began to walk.

'I saw Laurie in the street,' he said. 'She told me you'd had a row. She didn't say what about.'

Jess told him.

'Laurie's right,' he said. 'You've no proof.'

'So you're going to take her side!'

'I'm not taking any side.'

'You'd cover for Dave though, wouldn't you?' said Jess.

They stopped on the path and broke apart to face each other.

'He's my mate,' said Barney. 'Do you think I'd grass on him to Sammy? OK, so you had three cars burned out. Big deal! You'll get the money on the insurance. What do you think would happen to Dave if Sammy put the finger on him? He'd get kneecapped. He'd never walk straight again. Are you wanting that kind of revenge?'

'I'm not wanting any revenge. I don't want him beaten up.'

'What did you shove it in Laurie's face for, then? She's got enough to worry about over Dave as it is.'

'You seem to think you're the only ones to have worries! Do you think we don't because we've got more dosh than you? *I*'m worried about *my* brother too!'

'Hey, hey, calm down! What is this?'

'I don't know.' She calmed down. 'I guess we're all het up at the moment. The last thing I wanted to do was fall out with Laurie.'

'Make it up with her, then!'

'She called me a stuck-up bitch first!'

'For crying out loud!' said Barney. 'One of you's got to give in.'

Jess had to be getting back. They'd spent nearly the whole time arguing.

'I'll leave you up the hill.' He took her hand. 'It's time we started living dangerously!'

They went to the corner of her street and stopped within sight of her house.

'Nice place you've got there,' said Barney. 'Give me a kiss before you go.'

She kissed him and so didn't see her father's car coming up the hill. He pulled in at the kerb in front of them and lowered his window. Jess tried to disentangle herself from Barney but he, not realizing what was happening, pulled her back in towards him.

'It's my dad!' she hissed.

Barney dropped his arm quickly.

'Dad, this is Bernard,' she said.

'Hello, Bernard, how're you doing?' Tommy Magowan gave him a long, hard look. He'd know him the next time he saw him.

'All right.' Barney's throat sounded gravelly.

'You'll need to come in and pay us a visit one of these evenings.'

'Thanks.'

'Why not now?'

'Not tonight, Dad,' said Jess hastily. 'I've got homework to finish.'

'Another time, then.' He nodded to Barney and drove off.

'So, what about it?' asked Barney. 'Are you going to ask me in one of these days?'

'Don't be daft! It'd be a disaster. Dad would grill you till he'd squeezed everything out of you.'

'You mean about my father being in jail?' A note of aggression had come into Barney's voice. 'He wouldn't like that, would he?'

'Don't let's start any more arguments!' Jess gave him another quick good-night kiss. 'See you after school tomorrow.'

'Anyone phone?' she asked her mother when she came in.

'No one.'

Well, if Laurie could hold out, so could she.

She rang Neal.

'I could knock your heads together,' he said. 'You're so stubborn, the pair of you! If you don't make up, all that work on our song will be wasted.'

'"You are my friend for evermore!" Ha, flipping ha.'

'"Though our families fight their war,"' Neal went on. 'You're always moaning about your dad and his brother falling out. You're just as bad. You're doing the very same thing with Laurie.'

'She called me a stuck-up bitch!'

'Well, you are at times.' This was her cousin talking, her best-friend cousin!

'You've got a right cheek, Neal O'Shea. You're on her side because you fancy her!'

Everyone was against her!

Neal said he must go, he was going out. She had no time to ask him where or with whom before he said, 'Cheers!' and the line went dead. Jess thought she could guess whom he'd be going to meet.

Now Laurie was coming between her and Neal! Since she'd come into the picture Jess hadn't seen as much of him as she used to and when she did it was usually with Laurie. Maybe her father had been right – perish the thought! – that it was better to let sleeping dogs lie and not disturb them.

SIXTEEN

Laurie decided there was nothing else for it but to make another visit to Sammy. She waited until it was her mother's day off again and she was safely out of the way, at bingo with Granny Magowan.

On her way along to the Fish Bar she met Gregg and Jamieson lurking in a doorway. They asked her where Dave was and she shrugged. He was sitting in the house, had been all day, lying low, but she wasn't going to tell them that.

'We saw you the other night,' said Gregg. 'With your Fenian boyfriend.'

That gave her a jolt. How did he know about Neal? There could be only one answer to that. Damn that brother of hers and his big mouth!

She walked on.

Sammy's had just opened for business. There was the hiss and smell of frying. Betty was slapping the fish about in batter and Ena, the wee woman who sometimes came in to help, was setting the stuff out. The first customer had yet to arrive.

'Sammy in?' asked Laurie. He usually was at this time of day.

Betty nodded. The two women watched her going to his door and knocking. She kept her back to them. Once Sammy had had time to identify her through the spyhole he opened the door.

'Laurie, didn't expect a return visit so soon! C'mon in, girl!'

She went in and he closed the door.

'Have you reconsidered my offer? To help with your singing?'

'It's not that. It's Neal O'Shea.'

'Neal O'Shea?' Sammy stood with his arms akimbo, hands resting on his wide hips. He rocked a little on his feet. He was said to be in good shape physically. He went to the gym every morning before breakfast and worked out for an hour and he didn't smoke or drink. 'A clean liver', he called himself. Even went to church on Sunday. 'You're not saying you know Neal O'Shea, are you?'

'Yes, I am. I just wanted to tell you that you're wrong to suspect him of firing those cars at the garage.'

'The next thing you'll be telling me is that you were with him that night.'

'I was. The whole evening. We were standing together on the corner there when the fire engine went past.'

'Well, you don't say! When a man needs an alibi there's always some damn fool woman ready to give it to him.'

'I am not *giving* him an alibi. It's the truth, I swear it is.'

Sammy stared at her with those light-blue eyes that made her shiver inside. 'I think I believe you, Laurie,' he said slowly. 'You've an open face on you. An honest face.'

She felt her honest face heating up. The only thing she could think of now was escape.

'What does your da think about all this?' asked Sammy.

'He doesn't know.'

'He wouldn't be too thrilled if he did, would he?'

'Neal O'Shea and I are just friends.'

'Good friends, I hope?' said Sammy sarcastically.

'We play music together.'

'That's nice. Very nice.' He did a bit more rocking. Laurie felt he could pounce any moment, like a jungle cat leaping at its prey. 'Playing music, eh?'

She backed towards the door. She was glad to know the two women were in the shop. If she needed to she'd yell, though her throat was so dry she wasn't sure she would get any sound out. And would the women come if she did? Would they be too afraid of Sammy?

'Seems to me you are pretty sure about O'Shea.' Sammy pursed his lips. 'What else do you know about this business?'

'Nothing.'

'Are you sure?'

Sammy pounced then. He caught her by the arm as she tried to move away. He had hands like hams, fleshy and pink, but his fingers gripped like a vice. She gave a little yelp.

'I wonder now if that could be true? That you

know nothing.' Laurie felt the hot flow of his breath on her face. It smelt slightly perfumed, as if he'd been sucking boiled sweets. He had a weakness for sweets, her mother had told her. 'You wouldn't hold out on me now, would you, Laurie, not if you knew who done it?'

'Let go of my arm, please, Sammy! You're hurting me.'

He didn't slacken his grip. 'Tell me, who do you think might have done it?'

'I don't know.' She kept her eyes on the blue and red tattoos on his forearm. She had to focus on something. Anything but look into those eyes. She was afraid they might hypnotize her the way a cat did a bird when it stared it down.

'Come on now,' he said, letting his voice drop to a mere whisper. 'You'd better tell Sammy, hadn't you?'

'I've nothing to tell you!'

He let her go suddenly and she staggered back against the door. Her wrist was stained by an angry-looking red weal. She massaged it with her other hand.

'You'd no call to do that. I haven't done you any harm.'

'You've got nerve, I'll give you that, Laurie. More than your namby brother has. How's he doing, by the way? Haven't seen him about.'

She knew Sammy would be watching her face, waiting for every change of expression. He was trying to rile her into saying something she didn't want to say. He was no fool.

'OK,' he said, 'I'll take your word for Neal O'Shea.

I think you've told me the truth there, even if you're hiding something else from me. But I'll find the culprits, make no mistake about that!'

She opened the door and escaped.

When she met Neal that evening and he asked her how she'd got the marks on her wrist, she said she'd wrenched it. He took her hand in his to examine it and she winced even though his touch was gentle.

'Sorry!' he said. 'It's sore, isn't it? Don't know how you'd get marks like this by wrenching it. They look like fingermarks to me. Who did it, Laurie?'

'Nobody.'

'Somebody did. Wasn't Sammy, was it?'

She had to tell him and he was cross with her. 'He might have seriously hurt you.'

'I couldn't let you take the rap for Dave.' There, it was out! She'd acknowledged it. 'I'm pretty sure it was him,' she went on, feeling miserable. 'With Gregg and Jamieson.'

Neal had suspected as much himself. You didn't need to be much of a detective to put your finger on those three as suspects.

'Dave's not really bad, you know, just weak,' said Laurie. 'He's easily influenced. If Sammy finds out, think what he'll do to him!'

They sat in the shelter of the café for an hour, then Neal walked her home. He insisted. He was worried that she might run across Sammy.

'I don't want you coming past his shop,' she said, stopping a hundred yards or so short of her corner. 'Just leave me here.'

'Sure you'll be all right now?'

She nodded. 'It's great having you to talk to, Neal.'

'You can talk to me any time. You just have to say the word.'

He bent his head to kiss her and she didn't pull away. It was their first kiss, and it was as gentle as his touch.

'Good night, Laurie,' he said. 'Take care!'

'You too.'

He turned and headed off down the road. On the next corner he looked back and waved.

Instead of carrying on up the main road he decided to cut through the side streets to the Short Strand. There was no one about. About half-way along the first street he instinctively glanced back and saw two boys coming up behind him at a distance of about twenty yards. He recognized them. He'd seen them with Laurie's brother the night they'd been running from the shopkeeper.

He put on a spurt. He didn't run exactly but he did walk very fast. Power-walking, he believed it was called. He could be doing with some power! He heard them laugh. When he looked round again he saw that they were jogging, elbow to elbow, in an easygoing way as if they were out for a little exercise.

He broke into a run. He didn't have to look back to know that they were running too. He heard the drumming of their feet even above the hectic beat of his own heart and his thick breathing. He ran as fast as he could ever remember running. He turned a corner and saw the Mountpottinger Road ahead. It was a main artery where cars and buses travelled.

He was almost there when a stitch in his side pulled

him up. He had to catch his breath, and then they were on top of him, with booted feet and hard fists.

'Get off!' he screamed.

'Stay away from our girls, you Fenian bastard! Or you might not live to tell the tale.'

A boot found his head, and that was all he knew.

SEVENTEEN

The phone rang at one in the morning, wakening the whole household. Jess sat up, switching on her bedlight, looking at her watch. The ringing had stopped; one of her parents must have picked up the phone in their bedroom.

Her door opened. 'Jess, that was your Aunt Maureen,' said her mother. 'Neal's been hurt. Get up and come with me to the hospital!'

Jess shot like a rocket from her bed. 'What's happened to him?' she cried.

'He was attacked. That's all Maureen said. She was in a state.' Maeve shook her head. 'Who'd want to hurt a decent boy like Neal? I'm sure he's never done anyone any harm in his life.'

'Doesn't stop you getting attacked, does it?' said Jess. 'Being decent?'

They were on the road ten minutes later.

'Watch how you drive now!' Tommy called after them. 'I'm not wanting the two of you banged up as well.'

They were stopped at an army roadblock on the way into Belfast but once they'd identified themselves they were allowed to go on. The town itself was quiet. They were soon at the hospital.

Neal's mother was in a waiting room with Grandpa O'Shea. She was white-faced and when she embraced her sister-in-law her tears flowed.

'I was always afraid something like this would happen, Maeve. He's all I have.'

'There now, Maureen. I'm sure he's going to be all right.'

'How is he?' asked Jess.

'He was unconscious when they brought him in!'

'But not now?'

'He came round, thank God! Who'd do such a thing?' cried his mother.

'The streets aren't safe, sure they're not,' said another woman who was waiting. She went on to relate tales of all the people she knew who'd been beaten up, knifed, or otherwise had violence done to them.

'What the hell was he doing in a street like that?' demanded Grandpa. 'That's what I'd like to know.'

'He wouldn't hurt a fly,' said his mother.

'If I got the hold of them, see what I'd do to them!' Grandpa waved his stick in the air.

'Mind what you're doing with that stick, Father!' said Maeve.

Growling, he parked it between his legs. 'What are the police doing, tell me! Have they made an arrest?'

'They never do nothing, so they don't,' said the other woman. 'They're afraid to go into some areas.'

Then she shut up. It was always dangerous to go saying too much to strangers. She opened the magazine on her lap.

After they had been sitting for nearly an hour a nurse came in.

'How is he, nurse?' asked his mother, up on her feet.

'He's got three cracked ribs and a lot of bruising but, otherwise, he's not too bad.'

'Not too bad,' echoed his mother bleakly. How could cracked ribs and bruises not be bad?

'He's got some stitches in his head too,' added the nurse. 'We'll be keeping him in overnight for observation.' She went on to say that they could see him for a few minutes before he was taken to a ward.

The rest of the family had risen to its feet.

'You can't all four come, I'm afraid. He has sustained a head injury. Two visitors will be enough.'

'You go with your Aunt Maureen, Jess,' said her mother.

Grandpa was not pleased at being left behind but was smoothed down a little by the nurse promising to bring him a cup of tea.

'Three sugars!' he called after her.

'He's a sore trial to me at times, Jess,' said Aunt Maureen, as they went along the corridor. 'But after your Uncle Conal got killed I felt I had to take his father in.'

'That was good of you,' said Jess. It had saved them having to take him!

'And now this happening to Neal! It's all too much, so it is!'

Neal was lying on his back with his head wrapped in a bandage and a dressing plastered over his left cheek. His left eye was only a slit.

'You've been in the wars, haven't you, pal?' said Jess.

'You're not going to be left scarred, are you, son?' said Aunt Maureen, taking his hands in hers.

'It's all right, Mum, I'm going to live! And they can do great stitching these days, so the doctor told me.'

'What a fright I got when the police phoned!'

'I'm sorry.'

'*You*'re sorry! You've no need to be sorry. Who were they that did it? Did you get a good look at them?'

'Not really. Just know that there were two of them.'

He was lying, Jess could tell. She could always tell with Neal, for he was not a natural-born liar.

They stayed for only five minutes. They saw that he was exhausted and when he moved his head his eyes blanked with pain. The nurse came back.

'All being well, we'll let him out sometime tomorrow. But he'll need to take it easy for a few days.'

'Don't worry on that score, nurse!' said his mother. 'I'll see to it that he does.'

She kissed Neal good night and made way for Jess. As Jess bent to kiss him he said, barely moving his lips, 'Let Laurie know, will you?'

'What was he asking you there?' asked Aunt Maureen as they went back along the corridor.

'I couldn't quite make him out,' said Jess. She could lie more easily than Neal could.

She thought about Laurie in the car on the way home. She couldn't *not* phone her now that Neal had asked her to. They dropped Aunt Maureen and Grandpa off and carried on to Holywood, arriving there after three in the morning.

She didn't have the chance to phone Laurie until after school that day. She phoned her Aunt Maureen first, from a phone box, while Barney waited outside. Her aunt said Neal was home. Jess's father had collected him from the hospital at lunchtime.

'You can come and see him if you want, Jess. He was asking for you.'

Jess then dialled Laurie's number.

'Hi, it's me, Jess.' There was a silence at the other end. She went on, 'I'm really sorry to have to tell you this, Laurie, but Neal got beaten up last night.'

That broke the ice! Laurie melted straight away. She was very distressed.

'It's all my fault. If he hadn't been with me this wouldn't have happened.'

'If pigs could fly. It's not that simple, Laurie. I've been blaming myself too. I'm going to see him now. Do you want to come with me?'

'Do you think I could?'

'Yes!' said Jess.

Barney went with her to meet Laurie and escorted them to the edge of the Short Strand.

'Good luck!' he said.

The girls linked arms. They were friends again and neither of them had had to apologize!

‘That carry-on between us was stupid,’ said Jess.

‘It was!’ said Laurie. ‘I’ve been missing you.’

‘I’ve missed you too!’

Aunt Maureen opened the door to them. Her face dropped when she saw Laurie. ‘I hadn’t expected you to bring your friend, Jess.’ She said it as nicely as she could, which wasn’t too nice.

‘Laura wanted to see Neal.’

‘The doctor said he’d to be kept pretty quiet.’

‘We won’t be noisy, Aunt Maureen. Laura’s got a quiet voice, haven’t you?’ Jess thought Laurie was going to break into giggles.

They were allowed into the hall. Jess saw Laurie’s eyes flicker as they went to the statue on the wall of Jesus hanging from the cross. It was a distressing-looking statue, Jess had to admit that, with the body slack and broken and a bright-red heart bleeding on the chest. Gory, some might call it. A very Catholic sort of statue. Aunt Maureen had a lot of Catholic icons and pictures round the house, more than they did in theirs.

She opened the sitting-room door and reluctantly ushered them in.

Neal’s face lit up when he saw Laurie. Jess noticed it, and Aunt Maureen noticed it. Grandpa O’Shea was too busy eyeing Laurie to note Neal’s reaction. Jess introduced Laurie to her grandfather and they sat down.

Neal lay on a settee covered with a rug. The skin below his left eye was pouched and beginning to turn a dark mulberry and a sad yellow.

'What did Jess say your name was?' Grandpa asked Laurie, cupping his ear with his hand.

'I thought you were going next door to play dominoes with Dermot, Father?' said Aunt Maureen. 'He'll be waiting on you.'

'So he will.' Grandpa got up. Jess put his stick into his hand and helped him to the door.

'Maybe Jess and Laura would like a cup of coffee?' said Neal.

'Would you?' His mother was half up on her feet. 'It'd be no bother.'

'I could do with a cup,' said Jess. 'I'll give you a hand.'

She followed her aunt through to the kitchen, closing the sitting-room door behind them.

'Who is that girl, Jess?'

'Laura? She's just a girl.'

'There's something about her that makes me feel I should know her. Is she at school with you?'

'No.'

'What school does she go to?'

What school do you go to? Where do you live? What's your *name*? You could be pinned down by any of these questions, given an identity kit, put in a box and labelled.

Jess hesitated. Her aunt was waiting expectantly. She named the school.

'I see,' said Aunt Maureen, and that was Laurie in her box, tagged.

'Yes, she's a Protestant. It bothers you, I suppose?'

'Now you know I've nothing against Protestants, Jess –'

'Some don't even have horns!'
'It's just, well –'
'You'd rather she wasn't!'

EIGHTEEN

Jess cleared her throat loudly before returning to the sitting room with her aunt and the coffee. It gave Laurie time to get back to her chair from the settee.

'Here we are,' said Neal's mother in a bright voice, setting the tray on the coffee table. She poured the coffee and passed Laurie a cup. 'Shortbread, dear?'

'Mum's own make,' said Neal.

In that case, Laurie decided, she would have some, though normally she was not overly fond of shortbread, finding it too rich. 'It's fantastic,' she declared after the first bite.

'Your bandage looks as if it's gone a bit skewwhiff, Neal.' His mother tried to straighten it.

'I'm fine, Mum.' He moved his head out of her reach. 'Don't fuss.'

'We mothers can't help fussing, can we?' She gave a little laugh. 'I expect your mother's just the same, Laura?'

'Oh, yes.'

'She can't be as bad as mine!' said Jess.

'Still, where would you be without us!' said her aunt. 'Where is it you live, Laura?'

'Up near Holywood Arches,' said Jess quickly. It was near enough. Enough to mislead.

When they'd drunk the coffee and eaten the shortbread Laurie said she must be getting home.

'It was nice of you to come, Laura.' Neal's mother rose with alacrity.

'Come again,' said Neal, which drew another anxious smile from his mother.

Jess left with Laurie.

'That wasn't so bad, was it?'

'No, not so bad.' Laurie smiled, thinking of sitting beside Neal on the settee, with his arms around her and his hand stroking her hair.

'I think you're going all sloppy over that cousin of mine!'

Laurie smiled again. Then she thought of the statue of Jesus on the cross. She'd found the sight of it slightly unnerving.

'His mother seems a very devout woman?'

'Very.'

'And Neal?'

'He's not like her, but he does go to church.'

'Why did your dad change his religion, Jess?' asked Laurie. 'Did he ever tell you?'

'He said if we kids were going to be Catholic then he would too. To keep the family united.'

That was something Laurie couldn't imagine herself doing.

Jess asked if Neal had told her who had attacked him.
'The two we thought!'
The girls parted to go their separate ways.

Laurie called into the chip shop on her way past to pick up a fish supper.

'You'll never guess!' Her mother was agog. She leaned over the glass counter, keeping an eye on Sammy's door. She lowered her voice. 'Gregg and Jamieson got kneecapped.'

'You're joking!'

'Would I joke about a thing like that? Bobby Gregg's mother was in here an hour ago in a desperate state.'

'No wonder!' said Laurie. 'That's terrible.' The boys might be a pair of bad eggs, as Granny Magowan called them, but no one would wish kneecapping on them. It was a fearsome punishment.

For a brief moment Laurie wondered if friends of Neal might have done it in retaliation, but only for a moment. He'd be the last person to encourage anything like that.

'Who did it, do you know?'

Her mother nodded in Sammy's direction.

Laurie frowned. 'But what for?'

'The job at the garage, what do you think?'

Laurie felt sick now and the smell of the fish and chips was making her gorge rise. A customer came in and her mother had to serve. Laurie left.

'Don't forget your supper!' her mother shouted after her. She'd left it lying on the counter. She went back to collect the brown-paper parcel and hugged it against her chest for warmth. There was a chilly wind blowing in the street.

Dave was in his usual place hunched in front of the television set, gnawing at his fingernails.

'Have you been out today?' asked Laurie.

'Don't start all that up again! Why don't you go up Cave Hill and get some air, blah, blah!'

'I just wanted to know if you'd been out, that's all.'

'The answer's no.'

'You won't have heard then? That Gregg and Jamieson got kneecapped?'

Dave looked as if he might be about to throw up. Laurie pressed the 'off' button on the television set and killed it. She couldn't stand it being on all day, it gave her a dumb head.

'It was Sammy's men,' she said.

She had heard about seeing naked fear in someone's eyes but she hadn't seen it herself until now.

'Why did you do it, Dave?' she cried.

'Do what?'

'Come off it, don't lie to me! There's no point. You fired those cars with them, didn't you? *Didn't* you?'

'Lay off, Laurie,' he muttered.

'Do you think Sammy will lay off? You were mad, absolutely mad! You must have known you'd never get away with it.'

He had begun to shake and his face had taken on a deathly colour. He was frightened out of his wits! She put her hand on his arm, but he pushed her away and ran from the room. She heard him vomiting in the toilet.

She went to get a drink of water. She didn't feel

so good herself and she could smell chips on her hands. She washed them thoroughly under the tap.

The front-door bell startled her. Granny didn't ring the bell unless the door was locked. Laurie couldn't remember whether or not she'd turned the key when she came in. She should have done. Could it be Sammy's men come for Dave? She felt herself begin to shake. The bell rang again, shrilly and continuously, as if someone was leaning on the buzzer. She waited but it went on and on. She would have to answer it.

Slipping the chain into position on the back of the door, she opened it.

Sammy was standing on the step, with his arm resting against the bell. He removed it when he saw Laurie.

'I was wondering if youse were all deaf in there.'

Laurie was wondering why he had come himself. He didn't normally do his own dirty work.

'Is Dave in?' he asked.

'Not right now,' she managed to stammer.

'Away in and telling him I'm wanting a couple of minutes of his time if he can spare them. It's not worth his while him playing cat and mouse with me, you know that, Laurie.'

'Sammy, please, he was just being stupid –'

'Stupidity can't be allowed to pass. Otherwise people might think they can be stupid again. Sets a bad example. I won't lay a finger on him if he comes out.'

'Do you mean that?'

'I'm a man of my word. Not a finger. I'm just wanting to talk to him, reasonable like.'

'I'll ask him.'

'Tell him!'

She closed the door, leaving the chain on. Dave was standing in the middle of the living-room floor with his arms dangling and his head drooping. He looked like a floppy rag doll.

She told him of Sammy's terms.

'You don't believe him!'

'I think I do. He's not going to beat you up in the street.' Sammy wouldn't be the one to beat Dave up, anyway.

The doorbell shrieked again.

'He won't wait for ever, Dave. You'd better go.'

She propelled him out into the hall, hoping she was doing the right thing, fearful in case she was wrong. It felt like leading a lamb to the slaughter. Except that Dave was not an entirely innocent lamb. But innocent or not, he didn't deserve to be slaughtered.

She unhooked the chain and opened the door.

'Evening, Dave,' said Sammy. 'You're looking a bit under the weather. Either that, or you're scared out your socks? Come on out on to the pavement. I'm not going to eat you. I've already had chicken and chips for my supper.' He slapped his stomach and laughed.

Dave moved like a robot down the step.

'Just you shut the door now, Laurie.' Sammy wagged a thick finger at her. 'And don't be trying to eavesdrop. I wouldn't advise it. You and me are not wanting to fall out, are we?'

Laurie closed the door.

★

'We'll just take a wee walk down the street, Dave,' said Sammy. 'Make sure your sister's out of earshot. You know what women are like! Nosy devils!'

They walked slowly.

'Now I know you were in with Gregg and Jamieson over those garage fires so we'll not waste time going through all that. Agreed?'

Dave mumbled something.

'Shame what happened to them, isn't it? Real shame. You wouldn't want to end up like that, would you?'

Dave half grunted, half coughed. His legs felt like jelly.

'I've got a proposition for you. I might be prepared to let you off the hook if you'd do something for me in return. Fair's fair, that's what I say. You can't get anything for nothing.'

Dave thought of meat hooks in the butcher's shop, with bloody sides of meat hanging from them. He felt he could be sick again.

'Drugs, you mean?' he croaked.

'No, something else.' Sammy rummaged in his pocket and pulled out a bag of black and white striped balls. He offered it to Dave. 'Want a sweetie?'

'Er, no, thanks.'

Sammy popped one into his own mouth, replaced the bag in his pocket.

'You're good with cars, aren't you, Dave?' he said, moving the sweet into his cheek, where it bulged. 'You were quite a wild lad in your joyriding days. I've heard it said you could get anything going.'

'I don't know about that,' mumbled Dave.

'Taking a car would be nothing new for you.'

'I've never *stolen* one. Just borrowed like.'

'That's just splitting hairs.' Sammy shifted his sweet to the other cheek. 'This wee job for me shouldn't give you too much trouble. I'll give you till ten o'clock tomorrow night to do it. But that's all!'

NINETEEN

Laurie didn't believe Dave when he said that Sammy had let him off with a warning. She knew Sammy would be extracting some sort of price from him. But what? For once she could get nothing more out of Dave. He had closed up like a clam.

At least Neal had made considerable improvement and felt well enough to work again on their song. They were to have a final rehearsal and make the tape that evening. The deadline had suddenly come upon them. The next day, Friday, was the closing day for submissions.

Jess went to collect Neal and give him a hand with the four-deck tape recorder that he'd borrowed from a friend along the street. Laurie had decided not to come to the house. She didn't want to alarm Neal's mother any further.

Neal winced when he put his arms into his jacket.

'That garage is draughty,' fussed his mother. 'You'll get your death.'

'It's not pneumonia I have, Mum.'

Jess took his fiddle case in one hand and her guitar in the other, leaving him to carry the recorder.

'Don't worry, Aunt Maureen, I'll look after him.'

Her aunt watched from the door until they'd turned the corner.

Laurie was waiting for them there, huddled against the wall, sheltering from the wind and other dangers. She relaxed once they were inside the garage with the door locked.

Neal looked awkward while he was tuning his fiddle but he said his ribs weren't hurting, at least not much.

'Will you be all right?' asked Laurie anxiously.

'Sure.' He grinned. 'No choice anyway, is there?'

They started with the chorus. They all played the melody and Laurie sang.

'Two worlds in disarray
The secret broke away
Two worlds that belonged
And were silent for years.'

The secret broke away! Jess hoped the various secrets they were hoarding wouldn't break away. What a messy scene that would make!

'That was great!' said Neal.

Encouraged, they pushed on, working solidly, pausing only for hot chocolate, which Jess had brought in a flask. Time flew past.

Eventually, Neal said, 'We're going to have to record or we'll be here all night!'

He set up the tape recorder. They felt nervous now,

facing the final stage. Their first attempt was hopeless and left them groaning.

The next try was better, but still not good enough.

'OK, guys,' said Neal, 'let's do it again! And don't rush into it so much.'

This time they felt happier. The recording might not be perfect, but it sounded reasonable.

'After all, it's not a professional competition,' said Neal.

They listened again to the tape. They were so intent on listening that when someone rapped on the door they looked up, startled.

'Neal, it's Mum here.'

He had no option but to open the door to his mother. Her gaze zeroed straight in on Laurie.

'Oh, hello there! I didn't know you'd be here too.'

'Hello, Mrs O'Shea,' said Laurie.

Neal's mother addressed him now. 'Do you know it's half-eleven? You've been in here for *four* hours. That's downright asking for trouble! You're meant to be taking things easy, Neal.'

She then turned her attention to her niece. 'And how are you going to get home, Jess?'

Jess had missed the last train! And bus. She considered her options. She could walk. She was only kidding herself! Or she could borrow Neal's bike, but that would raise a dust, the idea of her cycling home in the dark with all the terrors that the night held. (She didn't really fancy it herself.) Or she could phone her father, which would also raise a dust.

'Your mum's already been on the phone, wanting to know where you were.'

Jess thought she detected a note of triumph in her aunt's voice. She probably reckoned she should be punished for her part in leading Neal astray. He had never been a rebellious son. How could he, when his father had been murdered?

'You'd better come up to the house, Jess, and phone your mother.'

They gathered up their gear and Neal slid their tape carefully into its box. He then handed it to Jess and she put it in her pocket. Neal's mother was standing her ground, her arms folded tightly across her chest. They could see she was determined not to let them out of her sight.

'I'll just go on.' Laurie edged towards the door.

'I'll leave you along the road,' said Neal, cutting her off.

'Neal, you're in no fit state!' said his mother, and indeed they could all see that he was flagging. His face looked sapped of energy.

'Laurie can't walk home on her own at this time of night,' he objected.

'I'll be all right, really I will.'

'You will not! I'm not going to let you.'

How were they going to resolve this? Jess could hardly ask her father to drop Laurie off when he came! She was resigned to the fact that he would have to come to collect her. He always told her to ring him if she was in a spot and he would come and pick her up. He didn't want her to run any risks. But when she did ring he arrived in a bad temper.

And they couldn't pick up a taxi. They didn't ply for hire the way they did on the mainland. Taxi drivers had always been easy targets for terrorists. You had to phone for a taxi and make sure you were getting the right outfit. Only certain ones would come into the Short Strand and then they wouldn't want to go near Laurie's street.

'Can you ride a bike, Laurie?' asked Jess.

Laurie hadn't ridden one for ages but was prepared to give it a go.

'She could borrow yours, couldn't she, Neal?'

He nodded. 'But we'll still walk you part of the way, Laurie,' he said firmly. He meant to the edge of the Short Strand.

His mother had the sense to realize that she wasn't going to win this one, so she shut up.

They all trudged along to the O'Shea house. Jess phoned her father while Neal lowered the seat on his bicycle for Laurie.

'Do you realize what time it is, madam?' That was Tommy Magowan's opening salvo to his daughter.

Jess was suitably apologetic and her father said he would leave straight away.

Neal and Jess set out with Laurie on the bicycle, watched from the window by Neal's mother and grandfather. Laurie went slowly, wobbling a little, with Neal keeping a hand on the back of the seat to help steady her. He looked more in need of steadying himself. Jess hoped he wouldn't collapse in the road.

When they reached the edge of the enclave Laurie said she would be all right now. 'It's not far.'

She put down the bike to kiss Neal good night. They lingered in each other's arms. They really had it bad, the two of them. Jess couldn't help feeling a little envious. She'd never been over-the-moon in love with anyone. She liked Barney a lot and found him great fun but she wasn't *in love* with him. Plenty of time to get serious about a boy, her mother was always telling her, and on this point Jess had to agree with her. She had too many other things to do with her life before she settled down. The thought of settling made her want to run. Now she could imagine Laurie marrying young and having a baby. She would make a good mother. She, Jess, could be its aunt! On both sides. That'd be a hoot. She could take it out for treats and pass it back when it started to yowl.

'Hey, break it up, you two!' she said. 'Dad'll be along any minute.'

And at that moment his car came into sight and drew up at the kerb. Laurie hopped back on the bike and took off at speed, zigzagging across the pavement as she went. Fortunately there were no pedestrians about. Tommy gazed after her curiously. The light was poor and Jess didn't think he'd recognized her.

They gave Neal a lift to his house and then headed home. Jess fell asleep in the car.

Next day, she went with Laurie to hand in the tape.

TWENTY

In the morning Danny had a coughing fit at breakfast and then his chest began to wheeze. He had to use his inhaler.

'I really don't think he should go to school, Tommy,' said Maeve.

'Oh, all right.' Tommy put up no resistance. His mind was elsewhere. He was thinking about his monthly payment to Sammy, due today, which he'd be able to pay only if a customer paid a large, overdue bill. 'I might be late tonight, Maeve. I'll give you a ring.' He departed.

'Your father's always worried these days,' said Maeve.

'That's business for you,' said Jess glibly.

She finished her breakfast and went for the school bus. Maeve got ready to go and open her shop.

'Will you be all right on your own, Danny?'

'Of course! I'm not a kid any longer!'

His chest had settled down and his colour returned.

'You could almost have gone to school,' said his mother.

'Too late now,' he said.

Dave awoke at ten o'clock. *Ten!* Twelve hours to go before Sammy's deadline. A dead line. It felt like facing a firing squad.

His mother opened the door and looked in on him. 'I'm just going to the shops. Are you getting up?'

'In a minute.'

'Are you feeling all right? You don't look too good.'

'I've got a sore head.' He didn't have to make it up.

His mother put her hand on his forehead. 'You're a bit hot and all. Maybe you should just stay put.'

That was what he wanted to do: stay put. And never have to move. He lay in bed with the curtains drawn, staring at the cracks on the ceiling. He could hear the sounds in the street, cars accelerating and decelerating, voices of men and women mingling, small kids shouting and squealing, some banging coming from further along where men were working.

He didn't want to steal a car. He didn't want to get caught, to go to prison. That was a mug's game. There was Barney's father rotting away in the jail. He'd gone down for a few years. Mind you, he'd done something more than just take a car.

Dave thought of getting his knees bashed into jelly. He put his hands over his knees, felt the hard bones lying close to the skin. He didn't want those bones pulped. He didn't want to walk on crutches for the rest of his life. Oh, God, what was he to do? He pulled his downie up over his head.

The front door banged as his father went out. Dave got up, dressed and went downstairs, sliding the chain on to the back of the door as he passed. Now he felt like a caged animal. He paced up and down the living room and banged his fist on the wall. He had to get out of here or he'd go nuts.

He ran back up the stairs to Laurie's room to see if she had left any money lying about. Opening the door, he was met by the sight of a bicycle squeezed in between the bed and the wall. Now whose could that be? Could O'Shea have lent it to her? It wasn't likely Laurie had nicked it.

He would borrow it, go for a run, get out of Belfast, away from Sammy's territory. He bumped the bike down the stairs and unhooked the chain from the door. Before emerging into the street he did a quick reconnaissance up the way and down the way. All clear. In a flash he was out and up on the saddle and pedalling fast, weaving his way in and out of the traffic, getting honked at but not caring.

He headed away from the town, up towards the Holywood Road. Why not go to Holywood? He liked being beside the sea. 'I do like to be beside the seaside!' His dad used to sing that. When they were younger, and his father was working, they'd spend whole days down at Bangor. They'd guddle about in the water, picnic on the sand, get chips for their tea afterwards up in the town, and come home on the bus when the sun was going down.

He felt free with the wind whipping back his hair

and the road flying by under his wheels. Only bicycle wheels. But that was all right. Today he'd no notion for a car.

The part of the coast he landed up on had no sands, only rocks. He didn't mind that either. He didn't mind anything as long as he was nowhere near Sammy. The sun was shining on the water.

He perched on a rock and spun stones through the waves. It was a long time since he'd spun stones but it seemed he'd kept his skill. It was one thing he was good at.

Danny had also been restless and taken out his bike. He cycled down through the town to the sea.

He met up with Dave on the coastal path.

'Danny!' said Dave. 'Not at school? Tut, tut!'

'Who wants to go to school?'

'Who indeed?'

'Whose is the bike?' Danny frowned. 'Looks like my cousin Neal's.' He recognized the saddlebag.

'Could be. I didn't nick it! He must have lent it to our Laurie. She had it in her room so I just took a loan of it.'

'Fancy going a run down to Bangor?' asked Danny.

'As long as your sister doesn't give me the blame again!'

'Don't worry, I'll see she doesn't.'

They cycled along the path to Bangor, where they parked the bikes, chaining them to a railing. They strolled round the marina, looking at the boats, and then they went along to Ballyholme, where they built a castle on the sands. They built it high, decorating it with shells and smooth stones, and made a moat all around it, which they filled with water fetched from the sea's edge in a rusted can.

Afterwards, Dave jumped up on top of it, shouting, 'I'm the king of the castle!' The sand caved in, taking the stones and shells with it. Danny joined Dave and between them they flattened the castle.

'Shame, in a way,' said Danny.

'It'd have got washed away any road,' said Dave.

They retraced their steps back into Bangor.

'What time is it?' asked Dave. He'd been asking at intervals.

'Six,' said Danny. 'Five to.' His mother would be home and wondering where he was, but he wasn't going to say to Dave that he'd have to ring his mum! He'd think he was a right baby.

'Six,' said Dave gloomily. 'Four hours to go!'

'Four hours to what?'

'Doomsday. I've been given an ult-im-at-um. Do you know what an ultimatum is?'

'Course. It's like a deadline.'

'You're right – a dead line.' Dave drew a finger across his throat. 'Got any dosh? I'm starved.'

Danny had some money in his jeans. They bought a pizza and walked along the front sharing it.

After that they drifted into an amusement arcade.

'Let's try our luck,' said Dave. 'I could be doing with some.'

They played the machines and for a while Dave was winning. He slammed the money straight back in, pounded angrily on the machine when he lost, and was threatened with eviction by the attendant. Dave growled but subsided.

They stayed in the arcade for a long time, watching the other players when their money ran out, and were surprised when they came out to find that it had grown dark.

'What time is it?' asked Dave.

Danny looked at his watch. 'Eight-thirty!' He really should be getting home. His mother would be climbing the wall.

'An hour and a half left!' said Dave.

'What's going to happen then? Tell me!'

But Dave didn't tell him. He merely drew the line across his throat again.

When they went to collect the bikes they found that they had gone!

'Where can they have got to?' cried Danny.

'Nicked,' said Dave gloomily.

'But they were padlocked!'

'You only need a good pair of wire-cutters.'

'What are we going to do? How are we going to get home?' Danny scavenged in his pocket, but they'd spent all the money he'd had.

'I dunno right now. We could take a look round for them but chances are they'll be a long way off by this time. There are pros who whip them away in vans. Fast as lightning, they work. Now you see them, now you don't!'

'Have you ever taken a bike? Not counting that one of Neal's.'

'Might have done.'

'You're not a pro, are you?'

'Me? No! I took a bike once so that I could go for a ride. And then I left it.'

'Have you never had a bike of your own?'

'When I was a wee lad. I used to crash it because I went too fast. I knocked my granny down one day. So they took it away and that was that. You know me – a right speed freak. Like yourself, eh?'

'Oh, yes!' said Danny, whose chest was beginning to wheeze.

'You OK?'

'I'll be fine. I just have to use my inhaler.'

'You should be getting home. It's a long walk but.'

'Maybe we could steal somebody else's bikes?' Dave's recklessness was beginning to infect Danny, to sprout in him like a seed. Anything was possible, wasn't it, if you decided to go for it? 'Just borrow them, I mean, not *keep* them.'

'We could, I suppose.' Dave didn't sound enthusiastic.

They had wandered away from the main thoroughfare and were in a quiet street of shuttered and grilled shops and dark offices. There was a line of parked cars on either side. Dave's eyes raked them as they went by.

Sudden spots of rain spattered their faces. They ducked into the shelter of a doorway as the rain gathered strength and swelled to a downpour. They watched, half mesmerized, as it bounced off the pavement. And then all of a sudden it stopped, as if someone in the heavens had turned off a tap. They blinked. The road glistened with wetness.

Near by, a clock struck nine.

An hour to go, thought Danny, to Dave's deadline.

'See that car,' said Dave, 'the second one along?'

'The Merc?'

'Aye. It's an expensive model. I'm going to take it for a spin. Into Belfast. You disappear, right? Go and ring your dad and ask him to come and fetch you. Don't tell him you've been with me.'

'I want to come with you! *Please*, Dave! I want to go for a joyride!'

'No, you don't. You go on home. This is going to be no joyride.'

'You're not *stealing* the car? For real?'

'This is real all right.'

'It's your ultimatum?'

'That's it! My dead line. To get me off a nasty hook. Now go, Danny!'

'I'm not going! Take me part of the way! You can drop me off in Holywood. You're a good driver, Dave, aren't you? You've said you are. *Please!*'

'Oh, all right!'

Danny kept watch while Dave picked the lock of the Mercedes. He did it in seconds and straight away reached inside the car to immobilize the alarm. He then lifted the bonnet and did something to the engine which started it purring.

'Right, get in if you're coming!'

Danny slid into the passenger seat. His hands were clammy and his breathing was tight.

'Smooth, eh?' said Dave, listening to the engine. 'Sweet.' They glided out from the kerb.

'Very sweet,' agreed Danny.

They had left the town behind and were heading

along the main road towards Belfast when Dave spotted a blue light in his mirror.

'Damn!' he said softly. 'Police!' He put his foot down on the accelerator.

Danny's mouth went dry. He held on to the loose seat belt with both hands. Neither he nor Dave had fastened their belts.

The police car turned on its siren and gave chase, with its blue light flashing. Dave kept his foot well down on the accelerator. The speedometer needle swung sharply to the right. Soon they were doing 90, then 100, then 105.

The road was greasy after the rain. They went into a spin. They were going to crash. Dave could see it all coming up. There was nothing he could do. Danny felt a scream fill his throat.

The world went black.

TWENTY-ONE

Laurie was standing on the doorstep just after ten o'clock, looking out into the wet street, when one of Sammy's men came round the corner. She could tell he was a henchman by his build; he looked like one of those American football players with their shoulder pads on. His heavy thighs moved slowly, as if they were rubbing against each other.

He stopped at the door, which didn't surprise her.

'I'm looking for Dave Magowan.'

'He's not in.'

'Don't give me that!'

'It's the truth.'

'Better get him.'

'I can't. He's not here and I don't know where he is.'

Laurie saw her mother coming round the corner. The Fish Bar must have shut early. Sometimes it did if business was slack. Beryl hurried when she saw her daughter standing with the man.

'What are you wanting?' she asked him as she drew level.

'Your son, Beryl. I haven't much time. Sammy's waiting on him. You know he's not very patient when he's kept waiting. He fidgets. They have an appointment, the two of them.'

'I've told him, Mum,' said Laurie, 'Dave's not here.'

'You can come in and see for yourself if you want,' said Beryl.

He came in. He pushed back the living-room door, as if he thought Dave might be hiding behind it. He looked in the scullery and the toilet and lumbered up the stairs, making the whole house shake. They heard him pulling things apart. Something splintered.

'If only your dad was in,' moaned Beryl.

'What could he do?' said Laurie.

They stood clear as the man came thundering back down the stairs.

'Sammy's not going to be one bit pleased about this!' he announced before he went crashing out through the vestibule into the street. They closed and locked the door and put on the chain. Laurie leaned her back against it.

'Mum,' she said, 'Dave was in on those fires at the garage. That's why Sammy is after him.'

'I was afraid that he was. I've been near out my mind with worrying. Thank God he wasn't here at any rate.'

'Wherever he is,' said Laurie.

The Tommy Magowan family was gathered in the sitting room debating what to do next.

Tommy had phoned the police an hour ago and

they'd told him that they'd had no reports of any boy or boys on bicycles being involved in an accident. They'd asked if Danny had ever gone off before without saying and his father had had to admit that he had, a couple of times, but never for as long as this. Had they checked with his friends? The problem was that Danny didn't have any close friends, though recently Jess had seen him speaking to a boy in the playground whose name was Brendan. Brendan who? She didn't know.

'He's thirteen, did you say?' said the police. 'Is he a wee lad?'

'No, he's tall for his age.'

'You know what these lads are like. They'll not stay in the house unless you chain them up. If he doesn't come back in an hour or two give us another call.'

In the hour that had elapsed Jess had gone out in the car with her father and toured the district. They'd asked neighbours. One of them vaguely remembered seeing Danny on a bike going down the hill, but that was all.

The clock in the hall chimed the half-hour.

'Half-ten,' said Maeve. 'I think you should call the police back, Tommy. Something's happened to Danny, I know it has!'

Tommy went to the phone and returned to say the police were sending someone along to take down particulars. And they'd asked if they could look out a photograph. Jess felt a chill in her heart at the thought of a photograph. For identification. What if Danny was lying murdered?

'Put a sock in it!' she told herself. Her mother had already rattled through a string of possible disasters.

Two constables came within ten minutes. Maeve described what Danny had been wearing and then broke down and cried. Jess put an arm round her.

'Can any of you think where he might have gone? Or if he might have been with anyone else?'

'Not as far as we know,' said Tommy.

Jess thought of Dave. She had thought of him before but had dismissed him from her mind. She decided to speak out now. 'He might just have been with another boy.'

'Why didn't you say so before?' demanded her father.

'It's only a vague possibility.'

'Any lead could be helpful,' said one of the constables. 'Can you give us the name of his friend?'

'Dave Magowan.'

'Dave Magowan?' repeated Tommy Magowan.

'A relative?' asked the constable.

'A cousin, actually,' said Jess.

'But the boys don't know each other,' said her mother. 'They only met in the shop that night.'

'They have spent a day together,' said Jess.

'Don't tell me Danny was with him the day he mitched school!' said Tommy. Light was beginning to dawn on him. 'If that's the case he might well have taken Danny away again!'

Jess tried to explain that Dave had not 'taken Danny away' but her words fell on blocked ears. Her father didn't want to listen.

'So,' said the constable, cutting off any more family

wrangles, 'can you give us a description of this Dave Magowan?'

Jess described him: thick, rather floppy fair hair, blue eyes, medium build. 'Looks a bit like Danny. They could almost be brothers, except that Danny is thinner.'

'Brothers!' That set her father off again.

'Calm down, Tommy,' said her mother. 'Watch your blood pressure.'

'It seems you have two boys to look out for now, officers,' said Tommy. 'You've still had no reports of any bicycle accidents, I take it?'

'The only accident we've had this evening was a joyriding one in Bangor. Couple of lads smashed themselves up. Skidded on the wet road.'

Jess thought her heart would stop.

'My son would never take a car,' said Tommy Magowan.

TWENTY-TWO

As soon as Jess had phoned, Laurie called a taxi and set off with her mother for the hospital, stopping at the pub to pick up her father. Ed Magowan was flabbergasted. He couldn't take any of it in.

'You say Dave was with *Tommy*'s son in the car? That couldn't be. How could it?'

'It just is,' said Laurie. She couldn't start in on a lot of explanations now. They were quiet for the rest of the way.

They were shown into a small side room at the hospital, where Jess and her parents were already seated. Jess jumped up and she and Laurie hugged and cried. Beryl and Maeve hesitated, then they too put their arms round each other and wept for their sons.

'This is an awful way to meet, Beryl, after all this time,' said Maeve.

'It's terrible, so it is, Maeve,' said Beryl.

The two brothers nodded in each other's direction and then stood with their feet planted apart, looking away. They looked like book ends. Lookalike book ends.

'Are they sure it's them?' asked Laurie.

'They fit the descriptions,' said Jess.

The two mothers started crying anew.

The door opened to admit a nurse. She was carrying clothes over her arm. There could be no question now of mistaken identity. She was followed by a doctor, who introduced himself. Their eyes were taken by the bloodstain on his white coat.

Tommy said, 'Just tell us the worst!'

It appeared that Danny's injuries were not life-threatening. He had a broken collarbone and three broken ribs. 'But those should mend fairly easily, at his age. He's pretty bruised, as you'd expect. It seems the car was travelling at a fair speed. He's been lucky.'

'Thank God,' said his mother, her fingers going to the cross that lay against her throat.

'You should be able to see him in a few minutes. The other lad's not been quite so lucky, I'm afraid.'

'Oh, no!' gasped Beryl.

Wasn't that typical of their family? thought Laurie. If there was bad luck going, it seemed to come to their door. Dave would have been the driver, so if anyone had to suffer it should be him, of course, not Danny, who was younger and an impressionable kid.

'Will he live?' asked Ed.

'It's too early to say, Mr Magowan, but we must be hopeful. He's in theatre now. He's got chest and head injuries, some internal damage too. We can't be sure yet what the full extent of his injuries are. But we've got great surgeons here, the best in the land. You can have faith in them.'

'Aye, they'll have had plenty of experience patching people up in this province,' said Ed bitterly.

The nurse and doctor left them.

'Why didn't I do more for the boy?' demanded Ed, turning to his wife. 'I've not been much of a father.'

'You did what you could,' she said, laying her hand on his arm.

'The boy's never had a chance but. No work. No hope. No nothing.'

'I'm sorry, Ed,' said Tommy. 'I really am. I know how you must be feeling. I've not been that great a father to my son either. He wasn't happy at school. He was being bullied. But I didn't listen.'

The two men were looking each other in the face for the first time. Tommy held out his hand and Ed took it.

The nurse returned to take Jess and her parents to see Danny.

He was in a four-bedded ward with curtains drawn round his bed. He lay propped against fat pillows, a surgical collar encircling his neck, his right arm in a sling and dressings half covering his face.

'Is Dave all right?' It was the first thing he asked.

They avoided the truth, saying they didn't know while Dave was still in the operating theatre.

They were allowed to stay with Danny only for a few minutes.

The other family was sitting as they'd left them, like three dumb statues in the stuffy little room.

'How's Danny?' asked Laurie.

'Bashed up but OK,' said Jess. 'He was asking for Dave.'

A nurse brought tea and suggested they go home. 'We'll ring you when there's news. There's nothing you can do here. It could be a few hours yet before he's out of theatre.'

'Hours,' echoed Beryl.

'These things can't be rushed, Mrs Magowan.'

'The nurse is right,' said Ed. 'We might as well go on home as sit here going round the twist.'

'Can we give you a lift?' offered Tommy.

'That's kind of you, Tommy,' said Beryl.

They managed to squash into the car. The four women went into the back, with Jess sitting on Laurie's knee since she was the lighter of the two. Ed sat beside his brother in the front.

'It's a lovely car, isn't it, Ed?' said Beryl.

Ed grunted.

The city was virtually deserted except for a couple of armoured cars on patrol. Nothing at all was moving in the Ed Magowans' street except for a greasy chip paper drifting along the gutter which made Laurie think of Sammy. At least Dave was safe from his clutches now. But at what a price!

'Would you like to come in for a cup of tea?' asked Beryl.

'Could you be bothered?' said Maeve.

'I'd like you to.'

'That's nice of you, isn't it, Tommy?'

'Aye,' he said.

He looked up and down the street before following

the others into the house. It was twenty years since he had entered it.

'Mother still in the same house?' he asked.

'Aye,' said Ed.

Laurie put on the kettle and her father lit the gas fire. They were all feeling shivery. Beryl made a pot of thick, dark tea and brought out biscuits which nobody could eat. The women did most of the talking. The men drank their tea and stared into the fire and said a word here and there when spoken to.

'Thanks for the tea,' said Tommy, setting down his cup. 'We must be going. It's late.'

'That was a lovely cup of tea, so it was, Beryl,' said Maeve. 'You must come to us sometime.'

Ed's family waved the visitors off from the door. It was three o'clock in the morning. Ed then went to bed, but Laurie and her mother dozed in a couple of armchairs, waiting for news from the hospital.

The phone rang at six. Dave had just come out of theatre and had survived the operation, though had not recovered consciousness. Laurie and Beryl were too exhausted almost to feel anything. They went to bed.

It was lunchtime when Laurie awoke. Her parents were still asleep. She rang the hospital and they said that Dave's condition remained critical but stable. She was making a cup of coffee when the doorbell rang.

Sammy was on the step. He gave her one of his sick smiles.

'I've come for Dave myself, Laurie,' he announced. 'Since he won't come to me.'

'You could have saved yourself,' she snapped. She

knew she was snapping but she didn't care. 'He's in hospital, unconscious. We don't know if he'll live or not.'

'What's happened?'

'He was in a car crash.'

'Was he driving like?' Sammy's question didn't seem as casual as it had sounded.

'Why do you ask?'

'I just wondered.'

Now Laurie was wondering. Sammy was reputed to deal in stolen cars. He'd deal in anything that could be sold.

'He'd taken the car. A Merc, the police said.' She saw Sammy's pale eyelids lift a fraction. 'Wouldn't have been for you, would it?'

'For *me*? Catch yourself on, girl! I'd never put a lad up to a thing like that and I wouldn't want you to be putting any such idea into the heads of any policemen. Tell your mother I'm sorry for her trouble.'

TWENTY-THREE

Granny Magowan came next. She was drinking strong tea to help her recover from the shock of the news when Jess and her father arrived. They were on their way up to the hospital and wondered if anyone would like a lift.

Laurie said she would. She hesitated, then added, 'Granny's here. Are you wanting to come in?'

Jess turned and looked at her father.

He sighed and said, 'I suppose we might as well.'

Laurie went in front of them into the living room.

'Granny, we've got visitors,' she announced. 'Uncle Tommy and Jess.'

Granny slopped her tea in the saucer and then busied herself pouring it back into the cup.

'Hello, Mother,' said Tommy.

'Hello, Tommy,' she said, looking up.

'How're you doing?'

'Not bad. Except for my veins.'

'It's been a while.'

'Aye.'

'Would you like to sit down?' said Laurie.

Jess and her father sat.

Tommy looked hot. He eased his collar away from his neck with his forefinger and swallowed. The collar was on the tight side.

'You've put on a bit beef, Tommy,' said his mother.

'Aye, well, in twenty years . . .' He coughed. 'Mother, this is my daughter, Jess.'

Jess regarded her grandmother for the first time in her life. She was wearing a fluffy pink cardigan buttoned across her chest and stiletto-heeled shoes and she looked as if she'd had her hair freshly permed. That was all Jess could take in.

'Hello,' she said. She could hardly call her Granny! She was a stranger to her, after all.

'You're the image of your mother,' said her grand-mother.

Jess realized that wouldn't be a compliment, coming from her, since she considered her mother to be some kind of temptress who'd lured her son away from their faith into the wickedness of Rome.

'They tell me you're in the money these days, Tommy,' said Granny. 'You've got a big garage?'

'I don't know as I could say I'm in the money exactly. Cash flow's a problem in the garage business. People aren't keen to pay their bills.' Fortunately yes-terday his outstanding bill had been settled, which had enabled him to pay Sammy.

'But you run a swish car, don't you? Laurie says she was in it last night. And I bet you've got a posh house somewhere.'

He shrugged. 'We live in Holywood.'

'All right for some!' Granny Magowan went on to lament about Uncle Ed being out of work and that Dave had never been able to find a job. 'And now there he is lying at death's door.'

'Don't say that!' said Laurie fiercely. 'He's going to get better.'

'Let's hope so,' said Granny in a voice that suggested she knew better.

'Aye, well,' said Tommy, and he rose, buttoning up his jacket, which indeed was a little tight over his stomach. 'We'll need to be on our way.' He half turned his back on his mother and took some notes from his wallet. He laid them on the mantelpiece. 'Just a wee something to help with the groceries, Mother.'

Granny nodded, as if it was no more than her due. 'You'll need to come to me for your tea one night.'

'Aye, right,' said Tommy.

'See you, Granny,' said Laurie.

'Goodbye,' said Jess, who had said only hello and goodbye to her.

Out on the pavement, her father let out his breath and his stomach, as if he'd been holding both in for the past while.

'She was never an easy woman.'

Jess couldn't help smiling.

He drove them to the hospital. Jess went with Laurie first of all to inquire about Dave.

'Little change yet,' the doctor told them. 'But it's early days. We found he had a bad hip break as well as his other injuries. We've done some repair work, but we'll need to do more later when he's stronger.'

'But is he going to be all right?' asked Laurie. Would

he live or die? And if he lived, would he be all right in the head? That was what she wanted to know. The doctors would still not commit themselves.

The girls were allowed to see Dave for a couple of minutes. Jess waited by the door while Laurie was at his bedside. Tubes stuck out of him in all directions. His limp hand lay on top of the coverlet and his eyes were closed, though the lids flickered a little. Laurie put her hand over his.

'Dave, it's me, Laurie. I don't know if you can hear me or not, but if you can I want you to listen. You're going to get better, right? I want you to get better. Mum and Dad want you to get better. We don't care what you've done. We love you, Dave.'

Jess felt her tears starting all over again. She gave Laurie a hug when she rejoined her in the corridor.

'He'll make it, Laurie. I'm sure he will.'

'I'm determined that he will!'

They moved along to Danny's ward. Tommy Magowan was at his bedside but on the point of leaving.

'Hang in there now, son. You're doing rightly. I'll see you soon.'

The girls settled themselves on chairs beside the bed and Jess unpacked a bag of fruit and chocolates and magazines. No car magazines, though!

'How's Dave?' he asked anxiously.

'Still unconscious,' said Laurie.

'It wasn't his fault, you know, Laurie, that I was there with him, in the car. You're not to blame him. He didn't want me to come. He told me to go home. It's true! I'm not just saying it.'

Laurie was pleased to hear that.

'I told Dad,' said Danny. 'Dave didn't want to take the car but he had to. To get himself off the hook, a nasty hook.'

'Sammy's hook!' said Laurie. 'But there's no point in going to the police. Sammy would just deny it. Anyway, he'd get back at us if we did. He gets away with murder, that man.'

Literally, Jess supposed.

After leaving the hospital the girls went into town to have coffee and a sandwich. Neither of them had eaten since the night before. They sat for a couple of hours, glad to be away from home or the hospital and to have some normal time. Normal girl-talk time. They talked about Neal and Barney. They always ended up talking about them.

'Barney's not had an easy time of it, has he,' said Jess, 'with his dad going to jail?'

'He told you about his dad?' Laurie was surprised.

'It's not the worst crime in the world, is it, taking a car? I don't mean I think it's OK, but that's what our two crazy brothers have just done!'

'Did he tell you why he took the car?'

Jess shook her head.

'It was a getaway car,' said Laurie. 'For a pub bombing up the Antrim Road. Three men got killed in it.'

'It would have been a Catholic pub, I suppose?' said Jess.

When Laurie told her which one, it almost knocked the breath out of her.

'Are you sure about that?'

'Dead sure.'

'That's the pub Neal's dad was killed in,' said Jess.
'No!' cried Laurie.

The secrets coming tumbling out were proving as difficult to handle as they had feared.

'Barney wasn't in the car,' said Laurie. 'He had nothing to do with it. He wouldn't. He's not wanting to follow in his father's footsteps, I know that.'

Jess believed her, but how could she continue to go out with him, knowing that his father had been involved in the killing of her uncle, her mother's brother, the father of her cousin and good friend? She and Neal didn't have secrets from each other. How could she keep this from him?

She was able to avoid Barney for a few days. Having to go up and down to the hospital gave her a good excuse. Danny was making rapid progress. Dave remained unconscious but holding his own.

She didn't want to see Barney until she'd decided what to do. It was so hard to take a decision! At nights the whole mess went round in her head like washing inside a tumble-dryer. But gradually she began to think she had no choice.

Coming out of the hospital one afternoon, the girls saw Barney waiting at the gate.

Laurie looked at Jess, and Jess nodded.

'I'll see you,' said Laurie and left them.

Jess and Barney started to walk.

'You've been avoiding me, haven't you?' he said.

'Possibly.'

'Why?'

'I really like being with you, Barney –'

'That is nice! I thought you hated it.'

'It's just that I'm too busy to see you regularly. To go steady. We've got our drama production coming up and then exams.'

'I've got exams as well. If I can find the time for you, you could find it for me. If you want to.'

'Maybe I don't want to, then.' There, it was out! She'd had to say it. There wasn't anything else she could have said. She couldn't tell him she was breaking off with him because his father had helped murder her uncle! That would be too much for him to carry. Better to let him think she was cooling off naturally.

'I'm not good enough for you, isn't that it?'

'Don't be silly!'

'You've never asked me to your house, have you?'

'You didn't ask me to yours, either!'

'You wouldn't want to come to a slum!'

'Oh, for goodness' sake!'

In a minute they'd be slagging each other off as if they were in a school playground. A primary school playground! But the heat they were generating was helping Jess to cope. To go through this in cold blood would be even more difficult.

Barney stopped in the middle of the pavement. 'I think I've got the message. I'm not that thick. You're fed up with me, you want rid of me! Go on, admit it!'

'All right, I admit it!'

'That's fine by me!' He turned on his heel and strode off without looking back. She watched till he had turned a corner and was out of sight.

She felt pained for him. It seemed unfair that he

should have to suffer for the sin of his father. But then, as their mother used to tell them when they were small, life wasn't fair. Jess felt she was only just coming to realize the full truth of it.

She felt pained for herself too. She would miss Barney.

TWENTY-FOUR

Since Dave's accident his mother was in a new, determined mood. She decided to give Sammy notice.

'It's time I had the guts to do it.'

Laurie went with her next day.

It was six o'clock and Beryl should have been at the Fish Bar at five. Laurie had had to play in a hockey match after school and her mother had waited for her.

Sammy was shaking salt and vinegar furiously over a fish supper. When he had wrapped it up and the customer had gone he came round from the back of the counter to confront Beryl and Laurie.

'Where have you been, Beryl? Were you at the hospital? Dave's no worse, I hope?' He put on what he considered to be his 'sweety' voice. Treacle, laced with acid, was how Laurie thought of it.

'As if you'd care!' said Beryl. 'It wouldn't have bothered you if he'd been left dead in the wreck!'

'You're maligning me now!' He wagged a finger at her.

'That'd be difficult. I've come to give you notice, Sammy. As of now.'

'Ach, you're having me on, woman. You're a right one for a joke.'

'This is no joke.'

'You wouldn't leave me in the lurch, would you?' This was a new experience for Sammy, somebody giving him notice! 'You've been with me a long time.'

'Too long. Do you think I'd go on working for someone who's ruined my son's life?'

'Hey, hey, Beryl, those are strong words! You should watch what you're saying!'

'Hey, hey, nothing! I'm fed up watching. Let's go, Laurie.'

He followed them to the door. 'You've forgot your overall!' he called after them.

'You can burn it!' Beryl called back.

'You were great, Mum!' said Laurie, linking arms with her.

'I'll miss the money, mind, but I'll look for something else.'

Laurie had a quick, selfish thought: the pressure on her would be even greater to leave school in the summer and find work. She was still determined, though, not to do it. She would look for a Saturday job, and she and Jess and Neal were going to try to get some gigs.

From Sammy's they went up to the hospital. Ed had been only twice; he didn't see the point of visiting when Dave wouldn't know him. Laurie had told him he should try to talk to Dave, about anything at all, and he had tried. 'Hello, son,' he'd said. He'd started to say something else, then he'd dried up and sat fidgeting.

Laurie and Beryl pulled chairs in close to Dave's bed.

'Say hello to him, Mum,' said Laurie. 'Tell him what you've just done! He'd like that.'

'Hello, son,' said his mother. She launched into the tale of how she'd given Sammy notice and as she warmed to her theme her voice strengthened and the words flew from her tongue. 'He needed to get his comeuppance from somebody,' she declared, sitting back. 'Even if it was only me.'

A little smile crossed Dave's lips. The doctor might have said it was a tremor but Laurie knew it was a smile. Then she talked to him, going over everything she had done that day or been thinking about.

'We're still waiting to hear about the song competition. Would you like me to sing our song to you?'

She glanced over at the duty nurse, who said, 'Go ahead! I'd like to hear it too.'

Laurie began to sing.

'You are my friend for evermore.
Though our families fight their war
Long for the day when there's hope –'

She broke off. Dave's eyelids were fluttering. They opened. The three women in the room held their breath and the nurse rose to her feet. His eyes closed again, and once more opened, and this time they stayed open. They were looking straight at Laurie.

'Laurie?' he said in an amazingly clear voice.

'Yes, it's me, Laurie.'

His gaze swivelled to his mother.

'Mum?'

'Yes, it's me, son.' She sounded as if she might choke.

Dave frowned. He seemed to be thinking. They waited. Then he said, 'The car crashed, didn't it?'

'Yes, it crashed,' said Laurie.

'Danny!' he cried suddenly. 'What happened to Danny?'

'He's all right,' said Laurie.

'Thank goodness.'

He was exhausted now.

Laurie phoned their local pub and got hold of her father. She told him that Dave had regained consciousness! He came at once in a taxi. They sat at Dave's bedside till he wakened again. He recognized his father and his father cleared his throat and wiped his eyes with his handkerchief and said, 'You're going to be all right now, son.'

And then Dave couldn't keep his eyes open any longer, so they left him to have a sleep, a deep, proper sleep.

When Laurie and Neal met that evening they both had something to smile about.

'I've got good news!' said Laurie.

'So have I!' said Neal. 'You first!'

She told him about Dave.

'That's the best news ever. Mine's nothing near as good. But it's quite nice all the same. Our song's got into the finals!'

'That's wonderful.' Laurie hugged him. 'But we've not been rehearsing.'

'We'll have to start again. As from tomorrow!'

When Laurie went home she found her father still in a daze over Dave's return to consciousness. He had all but written off his son's chances of recovery.

'It's like a miracle.'

'Maeve's been lighting candles for him in her church,' said Beryl.

There was a time when such information would have given Ed Magowan a heart attack. As it was, he looked a bit taken aback at the idea of his son being prayed for in a Roman Catholic church but he said nothing. It seemed to open a door for Laurie.

'Dad, you're probably not going to like this, but I don't want to keep any more secrets from you. I'm seeing Neal O'Shea, Jess's cousin.'

'Neal *O'Shea*! You never are!' It took a few seconds for Ed to get his breath back. 'Now look, Laurie, you can't do this to us! Haven't we trouble enough on our plate? Dave's not out the woods yet.'

'This needn't cause trouble, unless we let it.'

'That's easy to say!'

'But now that you've made it up with Uncle Tommy –'

'That doesn't mean we'd be happy for you to go the same way. Not at all.'

'I'm not going to go "the same way"!'

Beryl wasn't saying anything. She knew better than her husband when she would be wasting her breath.

'What about your granny?' demanded Ed, grabbing at straws. 'Think what it'll do to her! It could send her blood pressure through the roof! It could finish her.'

'She's old,' said Laurie, and he glared at her. 'Well, she is. And I can't help it if she's a stubborn old so-and-so. She's had her life. I want mine.'

'I never thought you could be so hard, Laurie.'

'I know this isn't easy for you, Dad.'

'*Easy?* What do you think my mates would say if they knew you were going out with a fella from the Short Strand? A Republican!'

'I'm sorry, Dad, but –' Laurie sighed.

'But what?'

'Neal and I care for each other.'

TWENTY-FIVE

They came second in the song-writing competition! They could scarcely believe it. They had rehearsed hard but hadn't really expected to be placed at all. So they won five hundred pounds, with the promise of an appearance on TV.

But winning wasn't the best thing about the evening.

Danny came to hear them, as did their parents, all five of them. They met beforehand and the two men went for a drink, leaving the women and Danny to come on into the hall. They were the first of the audience to arrive. They settled themselves in the front row.

'I hope the men won't stay too long in the pub,' said Maeve.

'I hope not indeed!' said Beryl.

Laurie and Jess thought it a good sign that their fathers wanted to go for a drink together. They had asked Granny Magowan and Grandpa O'Shea to come, but when they'd each heard that the other was being invited they'd both flatly refused. Their refusals had sounded dead flat, so the girls hadn't bothered to argue with them.

'The woman's a witch!' said Grandpa O'Shea.

'Sit beside that ould Fenian!' said Granny Magowan. 'I'd roast in hell first.'

Jess and Laurie imagined the two of them meeting, their backs arched, like two cats, ready to spit!

When Tommy showed up he was on his own.

'Where's Dad?' asked Laurie anxiously. 'He's not still in the pub, is he?'

'No, we've not been to the pub.' Jess thought her father had a cat-that's-got-the-cream look on him. 'He's outside,' he said. 'Come on and you'll see. Are you coming too, Danny?'

They followed him out, leaving Neal to look after the instruments. A wide blue van was parked at the kerb with Ed standing beside it. He also had a smile on his face. There was someone in the van.

'It's Dave!' cried Danny.

'It can't be,' said Laurie.

'It is,' said her father.

Dave was sitting in the front passenger space. He seemed unnaturally high up. When they went up to the van they saw that he was sitting in a wheelchair.

Tommy and Ed lifted the chair out of the van, taking care not to bump it. Danny dodged around, wanting to help. Dave kept his eyes down throughout the operation.

'He's embarrassed,' said Laurie softly. 'He'll not like being seen in a chair. It was brave of him to come.'

They set the chair on the pavement and Danny took hold of the handles. 'I'll do the driving,' he said, and grinned at Dave. Since going back to school, Danny had been finding himself regarded as something of a hero, which embarrassed him. He'd confessed to Jess that he'd been terrified when the police car gave chase and they'd gone into a skid. He'd thought he was going to die. But the three bully boys had stopped bothering him and he'd struck up a friendship with Brendan, the boy in his class.

'It's great to see you here, Dave!' said Jess.

'They've let me out for the night. I had to promise to behave myself but. Not to go too fast in my Ferrari! Vroom, vroom!' He pretended to spin the chair wheels. On Monday he was due to have another operation on his hip.

He'd been coping well in hospital. In a strange way he seemed not unhappy there. Laurie and Jess thought it was because he was removed from his problems for a while and was in a state of limbo. And he'd never had so much attention before, with everybody visiting him.

'We'll need to sing extra well now!' said Laurie.

'I've a feeling you're going to bring us luck, Dave!' said Jess.

And they thought it was because Dave was sitting there right in front of them that they lifted up their performance and did so well.

'This is for Dave,' Laurie said before she began to sing.

Afterwards, they all went out to Holywood and had a celebration.

Beryl was very impressed by the house. Ed became annoyed at her for keeping saying, 'Oh, look at that, Ed! It's like out of one of those glossy magazines.'

'You know I don't read magazines,' he said irritably. He gazed up the stairs. 'My brother's not short of a tenner or two, I'll grant you! He could slide a bit of it our way if he'd a mind.'

'Now, Ed, don't you dare ask him for anything! Laurie would kill you. And be nice to Neal!'

'What do you mean – be nice to Neal? Grovel at his feet?'

'Speak to him just! Instead of glowering at him!'

'I wasn't glowering.'

'Yes, you were!'

'Come on into the sitting room, everybody!' cried Maeve, breaking it up. 'We're going to toast the winners.'

Tommy proposed the toast, then he revealed that he had something else up his sleeve.

'When Dave's back on his feet again I'm going to take him on at the garage,' he announced.

Dave looked stunned. His face flushed and he didn't know what to say.

'Do you mean it?' he stammered eventually.

'Of course I mean it!'

'That's real good of you, Tommy,' said Beryl. 'Isn't it, Ed?'

'Very good,' muttered Ed.

'It's not good at all,' said Tommy. 'I hear Dave's brilliant with cars. A born natural.'

'Maybe our luck's beginning to turn,' said Laurie, smiling happily.

'If you're real lucky,' said Jess, 'I might even be your friend for evermore!'

They laughed and Laurie went to join Neal.

Jess thought of Barney, of the past and long, dark shadows. Could one ever escape them? Then she had a further thought: that when you move into the sun, shadows shorten.

The celebrations went on.